Proceed With Caution

Proceed With Caution

Pat Tucker

URBAN BOOKS

www.urbanbooks.net

URBAN SOUL is published by

Urban Books
10 Brennan Place
Deer Park, NY 11729

ISBN-13: 978-1-59983-054-4
ISBN-10: 1-59983-054-X

First Printing: August 2009
10 9 8 7 6 5 4 3 2 1

Printed in the United States of America

Proceed With
Caution

1

Naomi Payne pulled up and allowed the valets to park her car. She tugged the large straw hat down just a bit and adjusted the massive dark shades over her face. Rushing into the lobby, she walked up to the registration desk and whispered to the clerk, "Keys for Blair Smith?"

The clerk began banging on a keyboard. "Oh yes. Here you are."

Naomi took the card key and rushed toward the bank of elevators. She rode up to the thirty-fifth floor and let herself into the room. Once inside, she glanced around the luxurious VIP Grande Suite inside the Hyatt Regency in downtown Houston and could hardly believe she was there. The plush room was done in warm butterscotch and peach colors. Within minutes, she felt the stress all but evaporate from her body. She was excited about the pending rendezvous.

"Oh, damn, I better get ready." She pulled her gaze from all of the room's luxuries and glanced at her watch. He'd be there soon, so she needed to get ready. Naomi picked up her overnight bag and smiled as she looked around the suite one last time.

She sauntered toward a winding grand staircase that led to the bedroom. Naomi's stomach churned with nervousness and excitement at the same time; she always experienced those feelings when they got together. A quick glance at the king-sized bed and she was nearly left gasping for air.

"Oh my God!" she squealed as she picked up the dainty outfit. When her eyes scanned across the La Perla tags, her trembling fingers nearly dropped the teddy and matching robe. She remembered reading about the celebrities who wore the expensive brand and she nearly started hyperventilating. Calvin was so good to her.

The sound of voices brought an instant smile to Naomi's lips. *Calvin.* He was telling his security detail not to disturb him until he gave them the word.

"Yes, Mr. Davis."

She was surprised she had arrived before him. He had offered to send a car for her, but she decided to drive her own. He was always so generous and considerate of her well-being.

"I would feel better if you used the car service—"

"But I don't mind driving."

"I understand, but you said downtown was confusing to you. I don't want you to get lost."

"Sweetheart, just tell me which hotel, the room number, what time, and I'll be there."

Texas senator Calvin Davis was in his mid forties. But he looked like he was barely thirty-five. He was a statuesque six-two and 175 pounds. His chiseled features were dark and gave him a mysterious look. He had a short fade haircut and bronze skin. His smile was perfect and he spoke with such authority. Because of his movie star look the press had dubbed him "the Hollywood politician."

· He had quickly become the most important person in Naomi's life. Unlike with her previous relationships, which left her heartbroken and in the middle of unnecessary drama, Calvin treated her like a queen. Despite being a married father of two, he still managed to treat what they had together like more than just a fling.

Their relationship was supersecretive, because Senator Davis had recently been reelected to his fifth term in the Texas House on a well-publicized morality platform. He used to win by a landslide, but this past election was far too close for his taste. His challenger, Larry Armstrong, had been backed by the very man he beat for the seat in the first place. The mudslinging was fierce, but luckily Senator Davis had been walking a straight line. When he called to concede, Armstrong warned the senator that he should enjoy this victory because it would be his last.

Besides being a powerful married man, he was still a man and he was still weak, which to Naomi made him close to perfection.

Before Naomi could take a shower and slip into the silky lingerie, his voice was getting louder, which meant he was getting closer. She knew to keep quiet while he was on the phone, and she could tell he was.

"Tell them I'm no longer available, and have Vanessa do the interview!"

Naomi listened as he walked up the steps. Then she turned and he was there. As she met his gaze, she noticed a flicker of playfulness in his eyes. She shook off a shiver of arousal. She was so thrilled to finally be with him again. In that instant, she radiated happiness.

Because of his schedule, especially while the state legislature was in session, they had to share stolen moments when they could. A smile curled his lips when their eyes met, and she felt her heart melt.

"You made it!" He held out his arms to her, as if to beckon her closer.

"Yes, I just got here, and I didn't get lost." Naomi smiled. She couldn't help herself when she was with him, or in his presence.

She fell into his embrace, and soon his lips covered hers. Their tongues intertwined, and his quickly beat hers into a sweet submission. He held the back of her head and sucked her tongue and lips until he was satisfied.

When he pulled back, it was to unbutton his suit coat and loosen his silk tie. Then he removed his cuff links and his watch. Naomi watched him, then tore away his shirt and ran her fingers through the wild hairs on his chest. She inhaled his scent and closed her eyes, just thrilled to be able to touch him. He smiled, then pulled her wrap dress to the side until her breasts were completely exposed.

"God, I've missed you." His eyes traveled from her face to her breasts. They were all but calling out to him.

He lowered his head and took one of her stiffened nipples into his mouth. He tweaked it with his teeth, then ran his tongue back and forth over it.

Naomi threw her head back and pulled him closer. She was on fire, and needed him to set her soul at ease. Impulse caused her to rip the dress from her body. Calvin stepped back, giving her room to ease her nearly naked body onto the bed. In a frenzy, she shoved the lingerie to the side, crawled backward onto the bed, and watched with anticipation as he unzipped his fly.

"You're so damn beautiful, can't even think straight, always thinking about this juicy ass of yours!" He sounded breathless as he momentarily stared at her longingly.

She smiled up at him, giggled naughtily, then sexily turned onto her hands and knees and spread her legs, inviting him in.

There wasn't time to remove her panties, nor did he want to, so he pulled them to the side, and thrust himself into her.

"Ooooh yesss!" She bit into her bottom lip and moved her hips in a rhythm to match his deliciously wicked strokes.

He grabbed her hips, shoving himself deeper and deeper. His eyes bucked and he gritted his teeth as his muscle pulsated inside her slippery, tight tunnel, mixing a twinge of pain and pleasure together in a nearly perfect storm.

Naomi squeezed her eyes shut and screamed as a jolt of electricity raced through her veins; she was in euphoria, this she knew for sure.

"Ugh, I've missed you so much." His breathing had escalated to a fevered pitch. He grabbed her shoulders, pulling her toward him and moving his hips.

"Take it, Daddy, take it all!" This was what she dreamed of the moment they went their separate ways.

"Take it all, Daddy!"

He grunted and dipped his hips a bit lower. When

he felt his knees go weak he tried to control her movements, but she resisted, bucking her behind into his thrusts. And just a few strokes later, they were both in sweet ecstasy.

Naomi bit her lip to stop herself from crying out as wave after wave of pure bliss swept over her. Suddenly her knees began to wobble and gave way.

Naomi smiled, satisfied, as she lingered in that magical place. She wanted to ride the wave of ecstasy to the fullest. Calvin's touch was so electrifying; the sensation was so good to her it was nearly maddening.

2

Mondays after time with the senator were always so trying for Naomi, and this one was no exception. She still had her memories of the days before, but they were a source of frustration because she was left yearning for him even more.

Naomi took weary steps into the main office. She looked ragged, worn out, and downright depressed. Her normal cinnamon-hued skin was ashen, and lacked its normal glistening glow. There were dark circles beneath her doe-shaped brown eyes, her shoulder-length hair appeared uncombed, and her slender shoulders were slumped. She released a sigh, as if she were wrapping up, instead of just beginning, her workday. She made her way up to her classroom.

Soon her coworker, the ever so nosy Sheila Carson, breezed by Naomi's door and stopped instantly, sensing something wasn't right.

"Naomi? Girl, what's wrong with you?" Sheila whispered while her eyes darted around the floor. Before Naomi could raise her head high enough off her desk, Sheila had made herself comfortable by plopping down in the chair next to Naomi's desk.

"I'm just tired." Naomi shook her head as if no one could possibly understand the depth of her exhaustion.

"Girl, please do not tell me this is about your mystery man." Sheila's voice was laced with feigned concern. Her own pinched features were contorted into a frown.

"Nah, I'm just tired, really," Naomi said, exasperated. "I had such a busy weekend, I guess it just caught up with me." Naomi hoped that would be enough to satisfy Sheila, but a part of her knew it wouldn't.

"Sooo, did you see him this weekend?" Sheila's eyebrows inched upward. When Naomi didn't answer, she started giggling.

"I knew it! I knew it, the way you raced up outta here on Friday like your heels were on fire, girl, I had a feeling something was up. You've gotta tell me everything!"

"There really isn't anything to tell," Naomi answered somberly. "I'm just tired, that's all, and, well—"

Sheila reached over to stroke Naomi's back. "Girl, you've gotta get outta this slump. Besides, ever since you started seeing this mystery man of yours, who you can't even talk about, you've been acting all funny. Now c'mon, why don't you tell me about him, like what's going on?"

Naomi had been itching to share her secret with someone, but the truth was she really didn't know anyone all that well. She never knew her parents, and was raised by an elderly aunt who lived in

Alabama. When she had died a few years ago, Naomi packed up and moved to Houston after reading an article that said it was among the top cities in the country for blacks.

Naomi's aunt was very old-fashioned. She didn't like women to wear pants, or britches as she called them. She never married and never had any children. Each night, before bed, she had Naomi read the Bible to her. She worked as a domestic and believed in saving. So when she died, she was able to leave a meager inheritance for Naomi. That was the money she used for her move to Houston.

Sheila scanned the room, then eased back down.

"You can't be acting like this. Besides, girl, you look a hot mess, you don't need to be sitting around here sleeping on the job. You know, Diane is not in the mood today. If you don't look like you're getting ready for this in-service, she's bound to have a natural fit," Sheila warned.

Naomi and Sheila worked together at Ryan Middle School. Although this was a districtwide holiday for the students, the teachers and administrators were present for in-service. Their supervisor, Diane Roberts, ruled her department with an iron fist. She kept all of her subordinates, Naomi and Sheila included, living daily on the very edge of fear of unemployment.

Naomi and Sheila had met at work, and would occasionally hang out after work. But all of that changed when four months ago, Naomi lucked up and met the senator. He had been on a school tour talking about his new initiative.

At first Sheila was a bit jealous of the relationship, because Naomi was less available to hang out, but after a while she'd learned to take it in stride. But Sheila was a bit put off by the fact that Naomi appeared so secretive when it came to her mystery man.

Jingling keys announced Diane's arrival before Sheila or Naomi had a chance to pretend they were working.

"What is going on here? And, Carson, why aren't you guys in the cafeteria? We do not pay the two of you to be holed up in this room discussing nonwork-related matters," the older woman snarled.

Naomi looked up at Diane's graying mini Afro, her beady eyes, wide nose, and thin lips, with crow's-feet wrinkles fanning outward toward her flaring nostrils, and shivered.

"Diane . . . uh, I mean Ms. Roberts, I was just here helping Naomi. She's been having problems with the headset for her phone." Sheila snatched the phone from its cradle and hoped that would suffice.

Diane's eyes wandered between Sheila and Naomi. Then she looked at the phone that dangled from Sheila's hand. Her bushy eyebrows shot up. "It's broken?" Her voice dropped a few octaves.

Without uttering a word, Naomi looked up at her and quickly nodded.

"Umph," Diane grunted. She moved her wide frame all the way into the cubical. "Well, Payne, you should've called someone. Instead, you pulled Carson away from the meeting. Now I have two people down. That was not a smart move."

Naomi and Sheila stood by silently as Diane used a beefy arm to reach over Naomi without as much as an "excuse me" and plucked the device from Sheila's hand. "Lemme see what seems to be the problem."

"She says it's got this constant buzz when she takes a call." Sheila shrugged. "And we know how dangerous that could be."

Diane turned her head and glared at Sheila, then asked, "What are you? Her spokesperson or mouthpiece now? Let the chile speak for herself," she snapped.

"Yeah, it's buzzing," Naomi confirmed.

After a few moments of silent inspection, Diane unplugged the receiver and turned to her workers. "I'll be back," she hissed. The minute Diane was out of earshot, Sheila leaned closer to Naomi.

"Let's go to lunch so we can talk about your friend," she encouraged.

"I'm not sure if I can get away." Naomi knew she'd have to eventually say something. Sheila would keep badgering her until she gave up the business, but she knew she had to be careful. "Lunch sounds good."

Sheila's eyes grew wide. She stood and again glanced around the office, then sat back down.

"And we can talk about your mystery man?" Sheila rose from the chair and looked around the room again.

Naomi looked up at her through red eyes. "But you've gotta swear to me, not a word of what I tell you is ever repeated. Do you understand me?"

Sheila half shrugged her left shoulder. "Girl, who would I tell? Besides, it really looks like you could use a friend." She stepped out of Naomi's room and then quickly ducked back in. "I know we're talking at lunch, but just tell me, is it anyone I know?"

Naomi nodded. She watched as the hint of a smile curled the corners of Sheila's mouth.

"Remember, you can't say a word."

Sheila sucked her teeth. Her eyes suddenly widened. "Dang, this sounds big. Look, here comes Diane, I'll get with you later," she said before scurrying away from Naomi's classroom.

As Naomi sat alone at her desk, she wondered if she was making a huge mistake by letting someone into her secret world, then figured finally having someone to talk to could ease some of the frustration associated with being with the senator.

She had no way of knowing how that decision would forever change her life.

3

Naomi and Sheila were holed up in a corner inside Julia's. The restaurant was located just on the outskirts of downtown. It was always bustling with a lunch crowd during the weekdays, so they had to wait a bit for a table.

"So, who is he, how'd you guys meet, and how come everything has to be so hush-hush?" Sheila had asked the moment they sat. At first, Naomi was reluctant.

Naomi was crunching on croutons from her salad. She had already made up her mind to tell her, but still, something didn't feel quite right.

"You promise you won't say anything?" Naomi knew she was stalling, but she wasn't doing it on purpose. She just wasn't sure she could trust Sheila. Finally she said to hell with it and leaned in to get closer to Sheila, then stared deeply into her eyes.

"You can tell me." Sheila was getting a little tired of the games. She couldn't remember a time when she had wanted to know something quite as badly as this. Besides, she already knew Naomi was seeing

some married man. At times she marveled at just
how naive Naomi was. Did she think she was the
first woman to see some married guy who was
trying to have his cake and eat it too? Sheila figured
she'd humor her; then once she spilled the beans,
she'd have to teach her a thing or two, because she
had been there and done that so many times she
could be considered a pro. Sheila was only en-
grossed because her own problems had mush-
roomed into something she couldn't handle. Maybe
helping Naomi would somehow translate into helping herself.

Naomi swallowed hard, then sighed. "Okay—"
she began. "Remember a few months ago when the
district announced our school was gonna be used as
a backdrop for that political commercial?"

"Yeah, that senator, the Hollywood politician. He
was talking about Bibles in schools or something like
that." Sheila was hanging on Naomi's every word.

"Well, it's him." She eased back in her seat, trying
to gauge Sheila's reaction.

"It's him what?" Sheila frowned, confused.

"It's him. Senator Davis, that's who I'm seeing."
Again, Naomi waited for it to register in Sheila's
head. At first Sheila shook her head slowly; then her
mouth fell wide open.

"You're seeing Senator Davis?" She couldn't
begin to mask the disbelief. "But he's—" Sheila
began before stopping midsentence.

"You wanted to know my secret." Naomi continued to eat her salad in silence.

The moment it came out of her mouth, Sheila felt
like a fool. "He's married, with two kids, and—"

"See, that's why I didn't want to tell you. I don't need

you or anybody else judging me. It's just something that happened."

Sheila shook her head. "No, no, I'm not judging, but it's just, he's—" She shrugged.

"I know, I know everything you're gonna tell me about him, but I also know how he feels about me and how I feel about him."

Lunch continued without much more conversation. When the check came, they both reached for it.

"No, you paid last time," Sheila reminded her.

As they waited for their waitress, Sheila took a deep breath. "So, what's he like? I mean, in person."

Naomi's eyes lit up, and her smile stretched so wide it nearly touched each ear.

"He's wonderful. Our weekends are filled with such passion, and he's such a great listener." Naomi shook her head. "I've never felt so alive!"

"Sounds serious."

"I really think it is. I mean, I know he's got a family and all, but he's so good to me. I try to keep myself busy when we're not together, because I don't want to stress him in any way possible, I just want to be everything he wants in a woman. When he comes to me, I just let him relax and have his way. I take care of all his other needs."

"I can't believe you're seeing Senator Davis. He's so good looking. I mean, is he? You know, in person."

"You remember when he came by the school. Of course, girl, he's stop-traffic fine! You remember him, don't you?"

"Girrl, the way his security people were crawling all over the place, I didn't even get a good look at him." Sheila sighed.

Naomi sensed something wasn't right about

Sheila's questions. She wanted to tell herself she was just being paranoid, because this was the very first time she'd said out loud that she and the senator were involved.

"I know, it's surreal. But I think, I'm—" Naomi stopped speaking as Sheila's warning hand rose.

"Whoa! Affair 101, don't start catching feelings!" Sheila started shaking her head. "I'm serious. That's the fastest way to mess up your good thing. Take my word for it, I know from experience. It's not about love for these men, someone powerful like him?" She shrugged. "He can get love at home. Girl, the minute you start getting all soft and emotional, you might as well start preparing for the end."

Horror was all over Naomi's face. "Really?"

"Trust me. I know these things. If you really care about this man, you've gotta listen to what I'm telling you. Don't ever tell him how you feel. You just keep doing you and roll with whatever he sends your way, but don't go getting all emotional."

"But I can feel it when we're together, I mean, I just know he feels it too."

Sheila sucked her teeth and rolled her eyes. She couldn't believe what she was hearing. She knew Senator Davis had probably been married for more than fifteen years, so she figured he was just looking for a little something on the side. She'd have to school Naomi before the poor girl messed things up. "Look, I've been with a married man before, more than my share actually. And trust me when I tell you, the moment you start talking that love shit, you can kiss your man good-bye!"

Naomi took Sheila's words to heart. Maybe she had been too soft for the senator. The last thing she wanted to do was chase him away. She knew Sheila made a great point. The man was married, for goodness' sake! She never thought about his wife or their relationship, but she supposed it was true. The senator wasn't looking for love; he probably had lots of that at home with his wife and children.

No, she wouldn't start catching feelings, she'd keep it cute and make sure she gave the senator everything he needed except love. At that moment she decided she wouldn't ruin what they had by falling in love. Besides, Senator Davis was the best thing ever to happen to her, and she didn't want to do anything that might threaten their relationship.

4

Senator Davis, flanked by his aides and his security detail, strode across the rotunda inside the Texas state capitol. He had just wrapped up an interview about a new spiritually based bill he had introduced. "Did you call the driver?"

One of his aides, Matt, scurried to keep up. "Yes, but Beth said you wanted to go back to Houston."

"That's correct." The senator stopped at the capitol door. "You have a problem with that, Matt?"

"Oh no, Senator! I was just thinking you've been back for three days, and, if you go back to Houston today, well, you have a breakfast with the YFMAs Friday morning. That's the Young Future Ministers of America."

Senator Davis tossed Matt a scornful look. "I know who they are! What did I tell you guys about booking me for Friday events? I don't care what I have, send Vanessa instead." The senator walked through the door, but Matt's response halted him in his tracks.

"Yes, Senator, but this was an event that you booked personally."

The senator didn't like when he was forced to use his stern voice with his staff, but sometimes that's what was necessary. He wasn't about to stand there and debate his schedule or availability with his subordinate. He didn't want to meet with anyone but Naomi right now. When Matt didn't retreat, Senator Davis grinned and raised his eyebrows. "Notify the driver that we're going to the airport. Call my Houston office and tell them to prepare for my arrival. Is there anything else, Matt?"

"No. No, sir, that's it. I'll have Vanessa attend the breakfast in your place, then."

Senator Davis rushed down the stairs and into the backseat of his waiting town car. He didn't need to tell the driver a word; the car pulled away from the capitol and eased into traffic.

Memories of their last weekend together had haunted him since he left Houston, and he had to have more. When he strode into the house Sunday, his wife, Beverly, had had company.

"Darling, is that you?"

Who the hell else would it be at ten thirty on a Sunday night? he wondered as he entered the house. He wasn't really in the mood to entertain; he was drained from his sex-filled weekend, but that's the way he preferred it.

In hopes of avoiding an argument, he passed through the sitting room, just to show his face and be polite.

Beverly Davis was the epitome of a politician's wife. Her petite frame was always draped in Chanel sweater suits. Her mocha-colored skin looked its best because of specialty spa treatments and facials. She always looked well rested and refreshed. But with her, a smile was hard to come by, unless she was entertaining friends.

"Ladies." He smiled at the women gathered in the sitting room of their house. His wife stood and met him at the doorway.

"Good evening, Senator," one of the ladies greeted.

"We've been playing cards, sipping tea." Beverly offered up her cheek for her husband to peck.

"Don't let me disturb you all. I've got some work to get to, so I'll just see you when you're done entertaining."

"Okay, honey."

"Evening, Senator."

"Good evening, ladies."

Senator Davis rushed up the stairs and into his personal den. He hated when his wife had company. They reminded him of a bunch of old biddies sitting up gossiping and guzzling tea. He knew exactly what they spiked that tea with. The fine china cups didn't deter him one bit. Although Beverly was just a few months younger than him, she behaved so much older. The only sexual position she believed in was the missionary, she didn't believe in oral sex, and she felt women should remain quiet in bed no matter what.

Once he had tried to ask her about it, and just the discussion made her uncomfortable.

Once locked behind his doors, he began to daydream about Naomi. She was a tigress in bed, she loved trying new things, and at times he had to pull her off his stick. She enjoyed doing it.

That night, the senator slept in his study. Two

days later, he decided to stop torturing himself and made plans to see Naomi again.

As they pulled up to the regional airport, he got out of the car and walked up the tarmac. His personal assistant had already packed his bag and made sure it was stored away on the plane.

"You guys drinking?"

His security detail consisted of two burly men who hardly ever smiled, Derrick and Big Jim. When the senator asked the question, they exchanged glances and smirked.

"Of course you're not. Lucy, I'll have a martini. Dirty."

The flight attendant smiled and returned with the senator's drink. She also brought cranberry juice for the two men.

Senator Davis pulled out his BlackBerry and began barking into it.

"Vanessa, make sure the minibar is stocked in my room. Also let them know I'll need a personal concierge, because I don't want to be disturbed."

Once he was finished, he pressed the End button and eased back in his massive leather seat.

"The captain says we're cleared for takeoff," the flight attendant said. She closed the curtains and left the senator and the other passengers so she could buckle herself in the jump seat.

The forty-five-minute flight to Houston was smooth and fast, just the way he liked it. Once they landed, his security guys took the luggage and placed it in the trunk of the waiting town car.

As the car moved through traffic on 45, the senator could hardly contain his excitement. He wanted to remember the look on her face when he surprised her.

5

Naomi got the call while she was inside the Kroger Grocery Store on Montrose. She'd been walking up and down the aisles baffled about what she should have for dinner when the phone vibrated in her purse.

It was a call coming in from Lisa.

Senator Davis's number was listed under the name Lisa. Naomi didn't know anyone named Lisa, but just in case anything happened, she didn't want the senator's name programmed into her cell phone.

"Hi, baby!" Naomi smiled; she couldn't help herself. Every time she heard his voice, the butterflies sprang to life in the pit of her belly.

"I was wondering what you were doing tonight."

"Oh, I'm walking around the grocery store as we speak, trying to figure out what to eat for dinner tonight."

"Hmmm, dinner, huh?"

"Yep, sad to say, but I'm leaning toward the frozen section."

"Oh no!" the senator teased. "You can do better than that."

"Yeah, but that's easiest."

"Well, what if I joined you for dinner? Would that help?"

Silence.

"Hello? You still there?"

"Please don't play."

"Who's playing? I'm serious. I was calling to see if you'd like to have dinner with me."

"Tonight?"

"Tonight. What, you're not available?"

Naomi wanted to tell the senator she was always available for him, but Sheila's words rang out in her head. *"Affair 101, don't start catching feelings!"*

"Oh, sure, I'm free. But it's just such short notice."

When the senator didn't respond, her heart started racing. She hoped she didn't say the wrong thing. She didn't care if he called to say he was right outside her door, she'd always be ready for him. Panic began to settle in until he spoke up.

"Yes, but it couldn't be helped. I was held up in session. Otherwise I would've called earlier. I'm hoping you can find it in your heart to forgive me."

She knew he was joking, but his attempts always made her smile. "Am I coming to you or you to me?"

"I'm sending a car for you. How much time do you need? How about two hours?"

"Two hours? I'll be ready."

Naomi wanted to sing and dance around the grocery store the minute she ended the call. Here it was, just another ordinary Wednesday night, and the senator was making himself available for her. She immediately dropped her little basket and walked out of the store. She had only two hours to make herself presentable for his visit.

First things first. She dialed the after-hours recording for her school and left a message saying that she would be needing a substitute for the next day. There was no way she was going to work while the senator was in town.

After rushing home in record time, she pulled her closet door open and started scrutinizing her clothes. *What to wear, what to wear, something sexy.* Naomi pulled a royal-blue dress from a hanger and held it in front of her body in the full-length mirror. She and the senator didn't go out in public, and that was fine with her, but she wondered what he was planning. She hadn't expected him back from Austin so soon. The more she thought about it, she became giddy.

Naomi showered, changed, and fixed her hair. She decided on a burnt-orange one-shoulder dress. It was ruched in the front and swayed as she moved. After stepping into a pair of chocolate Marc Fisher stacked-heel sandals, she was ready to go.

Her cell seemed to ring right on time. It was Lisa again.

"Hello?"

"Hi, do you need more time?" the senator asked.

"Nope, I'm ready."

"Well, the driver is downstairs waiting."

Naomi grabbed her bag and headed for the door. She couldn't remember a time when she had felt so good about herself. She couldn't wait to share what she was certain was going to be another whirlwind evening with the senator.

On the car ride over, Naomi thought about her

relationship with the senator. While the rest of the world looked at him to make decisions and display his take-charge attitude, he didn't have to do that with her. She was his refuge. The senator never heard no from Naomi. She prided herself on that; there wasn't anything sexually she wouldn't do for him. Her number-one rule was never to discuss business with him. She wanted him to leave all of his work issues at the office, unless he wanted a listening ear. But that's all she did, she listened; she never once said, "Oh, you should do this, you should've handled it this way." His way was always the right way despite the outcome.

When he was with her, Naomi made sure the senator felt like a king. She'd dance and strip if that's what he wanted, or she'd rub his shoulders while humming to him by candlelight.

"We're at the Hyatt," the driver announced.

Once the car came to a complete stop, Naomi grabbed her clutch purse and waited for the driver to open her door. She pulled a twenty from her purse and offered it to him.

"That's not necessary, but I thank you."

She smiled, then entered the hotel and walked straight to the bank of elevators. She rode up to the thirty-fifth floor and checked her lipstick in a mirror. Everything was good to go.

Naomi stepped into a wonderland of candlelight the moment she opened the door to the VIP Grande Suite.

"You're finally here."

Naomi smiled.

"I hope you're hungry." The senator kissed her cheek, then placed a succulent kiss on her lips.

"I am, but not for food."

"In time. In time." Senator Davis took her by the hand and led her out to the terrace.

"Oh my—" A smile made its way to her face. She turned to the senator. "Oh, Calvin! This is so beautiful." She rushed out to the table. It was elegantly set for two, with fresh-cut roses as a centerpiece. A standing ice bucket was nearby and various hurricane candle holders were strategically placed all over the terrace. There was a mystical atmosphere in the air and Naomi wanted to show the senator just how much she appreciated his efforts.

"I knew you'd like it. Let me tell you what we're having for dinner."

Naomi watched as he strolled over to the table. He lifted one of the silver plate covers and said, "First we'll enjoy filet mignon, with lobster tails and potatoes."

"Ummm, sounds tasty." She couldn't wait to get to the senator. He always went out of his way to give her such sweet little surprises.

When he pulled her chair and she sat, soft music drifted through speakers she couldn't see. They dined and sipped champagne with the stars hanging above.

"This is so wonderful! I can't even begin to thank you enough for all of this."

"I know how you can start."

Before the senator could express his naughty thoughts, Naomi was in his lap. They kissed, first soft and tamed. Then things got a bit wild. They were tugging at each other's clothes, kissing and sucking each other as if traces of the champagne were oozing from their pores.

"I've missed you so much, Daddy." Naomi knew what her pouty voice did to him. The smile that curled his lips was enough for her to know he felt the same way.

Naomi stood and pulled her dress up around her hips. She kicked off her shoes, then eased down to her knees. The senator watched her with the eyes of an eagle. She opened his legs and moved between them. He laid his head back as she unzipped his fly and freed his member.

At first she started out by lathering it with soft and wet kisses. She had him right where she wanted; he was moaning, eyes closed, and clutching the arms of the chair.

"Jesus!"

The more he moaned, and squirmed, the tighter she squeezed his muscle between her jaws. She enjoyed giving him pleasure. Just listening to him had her so close, right on the very edge of orgasm.

6

Two Fridays after their last meeting Naomi arrived from work to find a black town car in front of her apartment building. Her heart nearly skipped a beat. The senator had told her it would be several weeks before he'd be able to visit again.

That car could be here for someone else. Every sleek black town car isn't one sent from the senator. She slowed her pace as she approached the car. She knew she should go into the building and mind her own business. But she at least wanted to see who would climb in or out of the car. Curiosity was eating away at her like crazy. After stalling as long as she could, she determined the car was in fact there for someone else, so she headed to the front door of her apartment building.

She had one step left before she could grab the handle.

"Excuse me, ma'am."

Naomi turned her head. Her heart skipped an entire beat, and she felt herself getting warm. "Yes?"

A uniformed man was standing near the car at

this point. She was close enough that she could see the car was empty, so she knew the senator hadn't dropped by to surprise her.

"I was sent here to pick you up."

Naomi's seductively arched brows jumped up on her face. Then the smile came. "Pick me up?"

The driver nodded. "Yes, I was told to bring you to the Sugar Land Regional Airport where you are to board a private plane."

Her eyes were wide, and the grin on her face reached from one end to the other. "Oh my god! Well, let me go upstairs and grab a bag."

The driver shook his head and said, "Not necessary."

Naomi glanced down at what she had worn to school that day. There was no way in hell she wanted the senator to see her dressed like that. There was nothing wrong with her clothes; they were clean, but they were also plain. And while she knew he would eventually see her in plain work clothes, as he had before, she liked to fix herself up when she knew they'd be together.

The driver walked to the back of the car and opened the door. "We should leave because traffic is sure to be thick this time of day, and you cannot be late."

Naomi looked toward her apartment building. Just ten minutes, that's all she needed. Then she looked at the open car door. She didn't want to miss that plane, nor her opportunity to see the senator again. But damn, she was wearing a pair of polyester slacks and a yellow button-down shirt, nothing spectacular. She didn't even have on heels, just her plain Naturalizer flats. "Just ten minutes?"

The driver simply shook his head.

Naomi dragged herself toward the backseat, climbed in, and crossed her arms at her chest. She didn't even have any makeup in her purse, just one tube of lipstick and some old press powder. *Oh well, that'll have to do*. She dug through the items in her purse and pulled out the compact. After dusting her face a couple of times, she replenished her lipstick and said to hell with it.

The Sugar Land Regional Airport was in far west Houston. The airport rented hangars for those who owned small aircraft and private jets.

When the driver arrived at the hangar that housed the Hawker 800XP, a midsized jet, he quickly opened the door so Naomi could step out. "This way, ma'am."

Naomi walked up the small stairway and onto the plane. The cabin had enough seats for eight. As she walked in, Naomi was able to stand without having to duck her head. She looked around and was a bit stunned when she realized she was alone.

She rushed to the door to say something to the driver, but by the time she looked out, his car was halfway down the tarmac. Naomi sucked her teeth and returned to the cabin.

Naomi sat on the sofa near the bathroom. She glanced around the aircraft and felt lonely. Why didn't the senator meet her on board? She had no idea where she was going, no luggage, and no company.

"This is great!" she snarled.

Her head turned when she heard footsteps. She looked up to see a flight attendant appear through sheer blue curtains.

"Hi, Ms. Smith, I'm Lucy. The pilot says we're clear for takeoff. Once we're in the air, I'd like to offer you a beverage. Is there anything in particular you'd like?"

"I could use a glass of wine."

"Is Chardonnay okay?"

Naomi nodded. When the flight attendant disappeared behind the curtains, she buckled her seat belt and leaned back on the plush leather sofa-style seat. She sighed and considered asking Lucy where they were headed, but decided against that.

It felt like minutes had passed when Naomi opened her eyes and rubbed them. She looked out the window and smiled wide.

From their descent, she could see miles and miles of white-sand beaches and crystal-clear water. She instantly became excited.

"Oh, good Lord!"

Just then Lucy came through the curtains. "You had fallen off to sleep, so I didn't bring the wine, but the pilot asked me to make sure you were ready for our landing. We'll be in Punta Cana in twenty minutes."

Naomi gave her a look that said she was confused.

Lucy chuckled. "Is this your first time in the Dominican Republic?"

"Yes." Naomi turned to glance out the window again. Lucy slipped back through the curtains.

An hour after they landed, a car was there to meet her. A uniformed man stood with a name card that read BLAIR SMITH.

Naomi smiled when she saw it. She looked around at the bright sunshine and instantly missed her shades. She climbed into the backseat and looked out the window as the driver left the small airport. She wondered when she was going to see the senator. It would've been nice to fly with him, but she figured that was a chance he couldn't take.

When the driver pulled up to a sign that read PUNTA CANA PRINCESS HOTEL, Naomi marveled at all of the coconut trees surrounding the property.

"Welcome to the world-renowned Bavaro Beach, home to the Punta Cana Princess Hotel." He held the door open for her to step out.

"Thank you!"

As Naomi walked up to the registration desk an elderly man approached her.

"Ms. Blair Smith?"

"Yes?" Naomi was a taken aback a bit.

"We've been expecting you. Please follow me to your suite."

Outside the door, the concierge said, "If you need anything else, please pick up the phone and dial the number twenty-five, and I'll be here momentarily."

"Thank you."

Naomi watched as he made his way down the hall, leaving her alone. She took a deep breath and opened the door. The room was massive, with a king-sized bed and a Jacuzzi in the corner adjacent to the French doors that led out to a terrace overlooking the beach.

She heard his voice and her heart began to warm. He was on the phone.

"I won't be available until late Sunday night."

She stepped into the room. Decorated in burnt orange and brown, it was inviting. The curtains were flapping in the wind from the open terrace doors. She could see the back of the senator's head as he held his BlackBerry up to his ear. A tropical drink sat on the table in front of him.

Naomi placed her purse on a nearby table. She had no idea how long he had been there, but the room looked lived in. She didn't really care either; she was just glad to be there with him.

She stepped out of her shoes, pulled her shirt from her waistline, and unbuttoned it down to her cleavage. She figured that was the least she could do. Instead of speaking, she stepped out to the terrace when he wrapped up his phone call and hugged him from behind.

"What took you so long?"

Naomi planted wet kisses along the side of his neck and up to his cheek. She inhaled, taking in his scent with her eyes closed, savoring everything about him. The aroma of salt water mixed with fresh air tickled her senses. She enjoyed his spontaneity. "I got here as fast as I could."

He ran his hands over hers, which were crossed at his chest.

"Hope you don't mind." He placed the phone on the table and picked up his drink. "I started without you."

"Don't mind at all." She smiled. When he moved the drink from his lips and extended it toward her, she sipped. "Ummmm, rum. Strong, babe."

"What's a drink if it's not nice and strong?"

He tugged on her arm, motioning for her to turn around and face him. "Let me see that beautiful face of yours in paradise."

When Naomi faced him, it wasn't for long. Their lips met and she fought to suck the alcohol from his tongue. He tore her shirt open and nibbled away at her breasts. After a few minutes, Naomi stepped away and stripped off the rest of her clothes.

"Wait, leave those on."

Naomi removed her hand from the waist of her panties. She looked down at the senator and his massive erection, pointing upward.

"He misses you."

She swung one leg over, pulled her panties to the side, and mounted him. Naomi was trying to ease her way down by wiggling her hips slowly at first, but the senator grabbed her shoulders and thrust himself upward to meet her warmth.

"Jeeesssus!"

"Ssssssss. Oh, Calvin!" Her eyes widened.

He stared deeply into them, wincing only when she tightened her walls around him. The senator moved his hips in just the right rhythm. He felt her body trembling badly. He brought her to a shuddering, wriggling climax that left her with stars and spots dancing in front of her eyes and her head spinning dizzily.

7

Another Monday after seeing the senator left Naomi even deeper in the dumps. She couldn't pull herself up out of misery no matter how hard she tried. She would give anything to be wrapped up in his strong embrace if only for a few extra mintues.

By lunch she was just outdone. Constant thoughts about what they'd done and how they did it just kept flashing through her head like a bad rerun.

"So, what happened this weekend?" Sheila asked as they walked out of the teachers' lounge.

"Oh my God! Sheila!" Naomi sighed, shaking her head.

"Damn, that good, huh?"

"You just don't know. He's so good to me, it's crazy. Trying to believe that this is my life is just so overwhelming sometimes, he's so good to me."

"You are so lucky!"

"I really, really am."

"Okay, girl, so dish it. I want all the juicy details. Don't even think about leaving out a single thing. Did you meet him somewhere? Or did he pick you up? Where'd y'all go? What'd you guys do when you got there? How does he act in public?"

Naomi threw her hand up. "Whoa! Hold up a sec, one question at a time, dang!"

"I know, I know, girl, it's just I am living vicariously through you at this point, you know I ain't had a date in ages. Let's just say the batteries have been working overtime. So forgive me if I seem a bit too anxious." Sheila laughed. "But the truth is, my coochie has been invaded by cobwebs long ago. I don't think I'd know what to do with a dick if it came knocking," she said, and Naomi started busting up.

"Well, let's see. I was in the grocery store when he called and told me to drop what I was doing because he was in town and he was sending a car for me."

"No!" Sheila's eyes were wide.

"Girl, yes!"

"Wow, just like that?"

"Just like that." Naomi told Sheila the entire story from beginning to end. She didn't leave out a thing. From the way the senator tried to avoid coming in her mouth to the way he bent her over the table on the terrace and took her from behind, with the wind as their blanket, she told it all. By the time she was done, Sheila sat stunned, but satisfied.

"Girl, just wow!" Sheila shook her head. "I mean, just wow, girl!"

"I know. And I know you say I shouldn't catch any feelings, but I gotta admit, girl, I'm falling hard and fast. And the way he treats me, I can't do anything to change the course I'm on."

"Well, lemme tell you this. I know you think it's all romantic and everything, but you've gotta be careful. You can't be available every time he calls," Sheila warned.

Naomi started getting worried. "Really? Why not?"

"You don't want him to think you're desperate. You know, like you don't have a life."

"But I don't!"

"He should never know that. I mean, think about it. Senator Davis could have any woman in the world he wants. What makes you think he'll want some needy chick who has nothing better to do than sit by the phone and wait for his calls? Every man loves a challenge. I don't care what they say, they all want to feel like you're a bit beyond their reach."

"Hmmmm," was Naomi's only response.

"Haven't you had people who liked you, and there was nothing really wrong with them, but for some reason there was just something you didn't like? Well, it's kind of like the same thing with you and the senator. If every time he calls you're jumping to his every whim, hmm, you won't keep him for long."

"But I thought having me when he wants would be a refreshing change."

"I could see why you'd think that, but look at it this way. You don't want your man getting bored because things got a little humdrum with you two, do you?"

"Absolutely not!"

"Well, that's all I'm saying."

"So what do you think I should do?" Naomi was really worried now. She had never thought of it the way Sheila did. She figured being with him whenever he called was just convenient because he had to split his time between Houston and Austin. Now the thought that her flexibility and availability could be the very things to ruin her relationship with the senator left her nearly overwhelmed with emotions.

"The next time the senator calls, don't take his call."

Naomi looked at Sheila as if she were speaking Arabic. "What?"

Sheila nodded.

"Don't answer his call?"

"That's right. Let him wonder about your whereabouts. Does he think he's the only man you see?"

"Uh, yeah, 'cause he is."

Sheila winced. "But he shouldn't know that. I mean, do you hear yourself? He's a married man with a family. You are single. So you telling me you're just supposed to sit by the phone and wait for him to call? What if he doesn't call? Does that mean you shouldn't have the company of a man because he's too busy for you?"

"Well, when you say it like that—"

"What? It sounds whacked, right?"

"Yeah, actually it does. I mean, you make it sound like he's just using me."

"If you think about it, he is to a certain extent. Look, I'm not trying to mess up this good thing you've got going. I'm actually trying to tell you how to protect it. You start dropping everything you're doing to run whenever he calls, he starts getting bored. Then next thing you know, he's got some other hoochie turning his head."

They arrived back at Naomi's classroom and she felt worse than she had before. She had no idea that being everything she thought Calvin wanted could somehow be detrimental to their relationship.

"Trust me on this one. You've got a good thing going here, I just want to make sure that you're not left out in the cold."

"I know, and I thank you for your advice, really I do."

Before she turned to leave, Sheila tossed her a knowing look. "Now what happens when he calls?"

"I don't have to worry about that, he's headed back to Austin," Naomi reported somberly.

"I understand that, but let's say he's sitting up in the capitol bored to pieces and his dick gets hard. He's, like, damn, I need to catch a red-eye to Houston so I can get my dick sucked. I need to call Naomi."

"Damn, Sheila, why you gotta make it sound like all that?" Naomi frowned.

"Because, that's how men think. I'm serious. It's all about a nut with them. I know this is kind of harsh, but it's the truth. So tell me, what are you gonna do?"

Naomi cast her stare downward, then mumbled, "I'll ignore his call."

"That's right. And trust me, you'll thank me for this later, I promise you!"

With that, Sheila spun on her heel and sashayed down the hall.

Naomi stood at her door long after her friend had turned the corner. Sheila had made a good point. She was single, but she didn't need to be desperately waiting by the phone for the senator or any other man, and that was a fact. Naomi decided at that moment that she'd take charge of her relationship.

8

Senator Davis had just finished fighting with his wife. He was sick and tired of her reckless spending. Twenty-five thousand dollars on a spa weekend with her friends was totally unacceptable.

"That bitch needs a job!" he snarled. He didn't like to do it, but he couldn't help himself. Each time Beverly did something to piss him off, and unfortunately lately she seemed to do these things more often, he compared her to Naomi.

Naomi would never dream of spending that kind of money. He loved the innocence about her most. When he did buy expensive gifts for her, like lingerie or the diamond bracelet he had yet to give her, she was truly grateful. Naomi didn't care about the power he wielded, she didn't care that he had a private jet, or that he wore expensive designer suits, she just wanted to enjoy her time with him, and he loved that about her too.

Where Beverly thought giving head would mess up her lipstick and expensive cosmetic dental work, he had to literally push Naomi off his dick. Beverly didn't think women should have to work in bed, but Naomi wasn't satisfied until they were both drenched in sweat. He couldn't stop thinking about her, and the way she made him feel.

"Senator Davis, a constituent is here to talk to you about the bill you authored." Matt stood in front of the senator's desk interrupting his thoughts of Naomi.

He looked up at the young man and wondered what his problem was. "Did she go through pre-screening?"

"Yes, she did. She said you personally invited her to drop in when she was in town."

Senator Davis sighed. Since when did people actually take advantage of his open-door policy? He only had it because very few voters actually dropped in on him. He started to tell Matt to deal with the woman, but decided against that. "Give me five minutes, then send her in."

The moment Matt closed the door to his office, the senator dialed Naomi's number. He was hoping to set up a phone sex date for later.

To his dismay, her voice mail came on. He held his BlackBerry out, to inspect it closer.

"What the hell?" He was about to hit the Redial button when there was a soft knock at his door.

"Uh, come in."

The door swung open and an elderly woman walked in.

"Senator Davis!" She greeted him with a massive smile.

The senator stood and offered her his hand.

She shook it. "Thanks for seeing me. I hope I didn't cause any problems by dropping by."

"Not at all, have a seat."

When she sat, the senator walked back behind his desk and took his seat. "So, what can I do for you today?"

"Senator, I want to talk to you about this Bible initiative. I know based on your platform how you feel about the lack of morality in our curriculum."

Senator Davis watched the woman's face. He even heard the words as they came out of her mouth, but that didn't stop him from tuning her out. Every so often, he'd nod his head, chuckle at something she'd say, or even pick up his pen to jot something down. His mind was spinning like crazy.

How come she didn't answer her phone? Naomi always took his calls no matter what time he called, or where she was; she always always answered his call.

"So you see why this bill is so important."

"Uh-huh."

Is she seeing someone else? What if there's another man in her life? She said she was single, said she was recovering from a horrible relationship and hadn't been with a man in nearly a year and a half. So how could she now be too busy to take his calls? What if she was lying up with some thug wannabe? He couldn't afford to take anything back home to Beverly; an STD would surely be the end of his career.

The more he thought about Naomi, the more he realized he really didn't know all that much about her. Sure, he knew she was a teacher who lived alone and was single. But he knew very little about her background, her family, and her dating life. When he thought about it, he couldn't believe just how careless he had been. But he knew for sure he wanted to keep Naomi, there was no question about that.

"I strongly believe—"

The senator rose from his chair, despite the strange look he got from his guest. "Uh, your name again?"

"Maybell Carter!" she answered, still looking at him strangely.

"Yes, yes, Ms. Carter." The senator extended a hand for her and she took it, getting up from the chair. "I'd like to thank you so much for your visit this afternoon, but I have another appointment. On your way out, I want you to see the gentleman Matt. He will take down your contact information and we'll be in touch."

"But, Senator Davis—"

"I can see how passionate you are about this, and I'm glad you cared enough to bring it to my attention. Again, make sure we get all of your contact information, and we'll be in touch." The senator guided her toward the door.

"But I was—"

"Yes, I understand." He touched her back and steered her to the door. "Don't forget, leave your information."

"Senator!"

Before she could finish her thought, the senator closed his door in her face and rushed back to his desk. He plucked his cell phone from his desk drawer and feverishly dialed Naomi's number.

Again, her voice mail picked up. He was fuming as he hit a button to redial her number. The outcome didn't change. He called four other times before his anger got the best of him and he slumped in his chair wondering what the hell was going on.

Maybe she was sick. Could she have been in an accident? How would he know if something did go wrong with her? Naomi couldn't, wouldn't have another man in her life. It was the main reason he had chosen her. He didn't want any problems. She knew the rules, she understood their relationship, and that's why things had worked out so well. It was driving him mad. The senator knew exactly what he had to do and he knew just whom to call to get it done.

9

Naomi and Sheila sat in her apartment. There was an awkward silence between them.

"So how many times did he call?"

Naomi said defiantly, "About a dozen."

Sheila looked at her for a moment. She was irritated that Naomi couldn't see this was for her own good. She sighed. "That's not too bad."

"But he hasn't called at all today." Naomi rose from the sofa and walked to the kitchen. "You want something to drink?"

"A glass of wine please."

Naomi pulled the refrigerator door open. Sheila got up and walked around the living room. This wasn't her first time at Naomi's place, but it was the longest she'd ever stayed. Usually she was dropping off or picking Naomi up. Sometimes she'd wait while Naomi finished dressing, but that never took more than five or ten minutes.

Sheila wandered around the living room looking at pictures on the mantel, and books on the shelves.

When Naomi come out of the kitchen Sheila made her way back to the sofa.

"Thanks," she said as she reached for the glass from Naomi. "I take it you don't feel too good about not taking his calls, right?"

"It just feels strange."

"I know, I know, but I hope you believe me when I tell you that doing it this way is for the best. I mean, this will make your relationship stronger. He'll respect you more, and value your time."

"Not answering his calls will make our relationship stronger?" Naomi snickered.

Sheila raised the glass to her lips. She cared for her friend, but oh, was she naive! Sheila said in a dismissive voice, "I know you don't see it now, but yes, actually it will."

Naomi's lips tightened, but she didn't respond.

Naomi wondered what was going through the senator's mind when he called and called and called and didn't get an answer. It had been torture for her to sit there and know he was reaching out to her and just ignore him. She fought with herself over it, but a part of her felt like Sheila knew what she was talking about, and she didn't want to lose the senator. She convinced herself that being less available would definitely strengthen what they had.

Naomi finally turned to face Sheila. "To be honest with you, I don't feel comfortable ignoring him like this. I mean, I can't help but think he didn't call today because he was mad."

Sheila shook her head. Oh, this girl had so much to learn. "I remember the last married man I dated."

Naomi perked up a bit. Now Sheila had her attention.

"I loved him, I really did. I thought he'd leave his

wife for me. I mean, after all, he wasn't happy with her anyway, so why stay? No one stays just for the kids these days. I made him happy, he made me happy, so why couldn't we be together permanently?" Sheila sipped her wine. It was clear the memory was causing her to be emotional.

"We would've been perfect together. I did every- and anything as long as I thought it might make him happy. Girl, we had sex all over the place, public restrooms, in the car, the park."

Naomi's eyes grew wide. "So what happened to y'all?" She wanted to know.

"I changed my entire life around for him. I wouldn't leave the house after seven in the evening because I didn't want to miss his calls. He'd set dates with me, and then his wife would decide she wanted to do something and I'd be left high and dry. He even told me he didn't want me giving out my number to other men. Basically he isolated me from my family and friends, and soon I wasn't doing any- thing unless he knew about it and approved."

"Really?"

Sheila nodded. "Yes, girl. I had it bad. We were together for three years. I really thought he'd leave her ass. He talked about her so bad, I couldn't un- derstand why he'd stay."

"Did you ever ask him to leave her?"

"At first I wouldn't. I'd just cook for him, rub his back and feet when he was tired. I tried not to pout or cry when in the middle of the night he had to go home, but the shit used to piss me off. See, with you and the senator it's different. He actually spends the night with you."

"He does."

"But, girl, imagine, you just got through rocking his world, y'all lying up in the afterglow of some fabulous spine-tingling sex and you ready to cuddle up next to your man and drift into a blissful sleep, when he eases himself away from you and kisses you on the forehead, talking about, 'I'll call you soon.'"

The horror on Naomi's face couldn't begin to really express how she felt. As Sheila spoke the words, she kept thinking of herself and the senator. "What do you think was your biggest mistake?"

"I thought about that for a long time. I really believe the fact that he was my everything was my downfall. I mean, if I had a life outside of him, if every once in a while he had to wonder where I was, maybe he would've respected what we had more."

"I just never thought about it like that." Naomi drained her glass. "You want another drink?"

Sheila took hers to the head and gave her glass to Naomi.

"You miss him?"

"Sometimes. We were in love, I really believe that. I don't think it's impossible to love more than one person at a time, but I still think I made my mistake when I wrapped my entire world around him."

From the kitchen, Naomi was listening to Sheila, but her mind was really on her own relationship with the senator. He was more experienced, he had all the advantages, he had all the control. Things had to change. There was no way in hell she'd wind up like Sheila, bitter and alone.

No, she'd be different from the typical mistress. When it was all said and done, she and her senator would be together. Enough of this "stolen moment" stuff.

10

In his office in Austin, Senator Davis was watching the scene play out in Naomi's apartment. The small monitor was portable, but he had had it installed behind the bookcase in his office. Big Jim, one of his security aides, stood next to him.

"I hope you believe me when I tell you that doing it this way is for the best. I mean, this will make your relationship stronger. He'll respect you more, and value your time."

"Not answering his calls will make our relationship stronger?"

Naomi's apartment had been wired with state-of-the-art monitoring equipment. The senator made sure Big Jim understood he wanted cutting-edge technology that was portable. There were TV screens and audio equipment in every room of the apartment. Her cell phone was replaced with an exact replica, except the new one had a microchip similar to a Global Positioning System that tracked her calls and monitored her whereabouts. The Web-based camera was the size of a button and enabled the

senator to track movement and sound anywhere in
the country. For an extra fee he also had international
options as well. The shed in the backyard housed
the server that serviced the cameras and audio
equipment. Since there was a wireless modem, the
equipment could be accessed from various satellites
just like a cell phone.

"Are you satisfied?"

"Yes. This is good. Your men did a great job."

"What about Sheila's place?"

"Not yet. But keep a close eye on her. I'm not
sure we need to be too concerned about her just yet.
But for now this is good."

"You got it, boss."

Big Jim nodded, then walked out of the office.

Jim Blake would look out for his interests; that
much the senator knew. He leaned back with confi-
dence in Jim's abilities. Years ago while he was speaking at an event in the third ward, Jim had waited for
him backstage.

"Mr. Davis, you grew up with my dad," he
had said.

"Oh?"

"Yeah. Jim Cool-hand Blake. I'm his son."

The senator stopped and listened to the burly man
who stood in front of him. "Cool-hand Jim. Yeah, I
remember him. So you say you're his son, huh?"

"Yeah, and I was wondering if you ever need any
kinda work done. I'm good with my hands, real fast
on my feet."

Senator Davis had been a freshman back then,
fresh off his first victory beating out a twenty-nine-
year incumbent. He had received a dozen death
threats. He sized Jim up; he was a big brawny man,

muscular and bald. "You ever been up to that gated community?"

"Yessir, but I did my time like a man. Boys around the block put a bullet through my ol' man's head. I couldn't just let that ride," Jim said.

"You mean to tell me Cool-hand Jim is dead?" Senator Davis was horrified. He and Jim's dad had gone way back together. They ran the streets of Houston's third and fifth wards, looking for hot women and trouble. Those were the days, the senator thought; he had fond memories of his time with Cool-hand Jim.

"I was just wondering if you had any heavy lifting or anything you needed some muscle for. I'm your man. My pops used ta talk about you all the time."

Senator Davis pulled a card from his breast pocket and scribbled his cell number on the back. "I want you to call me Tuesday morning at nine fifteen. Don't be late!" he said as his handlers rushed him into a black Suburban with tinted windows.

Two weeks later, Big Jim Blake was a member of the senator's personal security detail and he'd been at his side ever since. Big Jim knew how to handle things discreetly, and best of all, the senator never had to get his hands dirty.

When the senator needed things done, if Big Jim couldn't do it, he knew someone who could. Their work relationship had blossomed into a strong friendship.

Once he was alone, the senator kept looking at the screen. He wondered why Naomi was listening to this woman, but most importantly he wondered what the woman's agenda was. He made a mental note to find out everything he could about this Sheila.

He didn't feel threatened by her influence over Naomi, but he wanted to make sure he stayed on top of things before they got out of control. The senator didn't believe in reacting after the damage was done; he liked to anticipate things before they occurred, then find a way to head them off before they got out of hand. That was his style. And no matter how much he tried to calm himself, something told him Sheila was one to watch. And once someone was on his radar, that usually meant trouble was right around the corner.

11

Naomi was teetering on the very edge of insanity. She had no idea what she should do. All she knew was it had been two long lonely weeks since the senator had called and she was sick. The number she had for him was nothing but a voice-mail box. She had been played, but the problem was she had done exactly what Sheila warned her against.

"Affair 101, don't start catching feelings!"

As she paced back and forth in her living room she wondered what she could do to make things right again. She plucked the phone from its cradle and used shaky fingers to dial Sheila's number. She didn't know what else to do.

The moment Sheila said hello, Naomi started ranting and raving. "I haven't heard from him in weeks. I'm dying. I don't know what to do. You said not answering his calls would make him want me more. Why isn't he calling?"

"Calm down!" Sheila yelled.

"Don't tell me to calm down, I'm about to lose

my fuckin' mind. He's not calling, he's not taking my calls, and you're telling me to calm down?"

"Naomi, yelling at me ain't gonna help."

"Well, tell me what the hell will. You told me not to take his calls. You said it would make him respect me, love me even more, but now I'm alone, Sheila. Alone!"

"I'm coming over!"

Naomi dropped the phone and started bawling. Her shoulders convulsed and she fell to the floor, crying harder than she ever had before.

By the time there was a knock at her door, she didn't know if it was the pounding in her head or someone trying to get in. Her head snapped toward the door. Maybe it was his driver; he had come for her to collect her and take her to the Hyatt downtown.

Naomi rose and tried her best to straighten her clothes where she stood. She used the back of her hand to dry her wet face. After sniffling a couple of times, she plastered on the best smile she could and headed for the front door. Before grabbing the handle, she took a deep breath and pulled the door open. The smile she had forced vanished at the sight of Sheila.

"Oh God! Are you okay?"

Unable to find words to form an answer, Naomi turned and walked away from the door. Before stepping in, Sheila glanced around in both directions, then entered the apartment and closed the door. She locked it before she rushed to Naomi's side.

"It's gonna be okay. Do you want something to drink?" Sheila asked.

"No, I want Calvin back," Naomi sobbed. She fell into Sheila's arms.

"I know, honey, I know. But trust me when I say if it's over, it's best it happened now."

Suddenly Naomi stopped crying and pulled herself away from Sheila. She looked at her, frowned, and said, "I don't think you understand. I'm nothing without him, nothing!"

"That's not true," Sheila said.

"Look at me, look around. My life meant nothing until he came into it. It's just that simple." Tears streamed down her cheeks again. "And now that he's gone, I'm back to nothing again."

Sheila stood. "That's it. We're going out and we're gonna have ourselves a good time. Before long, you won't even think about the senator anymore!" she announced.

Naomi looked up at her through red puffy eyes. Sheila had gone and lost her mind, she thought. "Going out? Are you crazy? I'm not going anywhere. What if he calls and I'm off getting my groove on? He'll never take me back at that point."

"That's not the way to get over this man, it's not the way to get him back."

Naomi was starting to get angry with herself. She had listened to everything Sheila said, and now, just like Sheila, she was alone. There was no way in hell she was going to some meat market of a bar so men could pass her up for scantily dressed hoochies. She didn't need that shit. What she needed was the senator, and no one else, nothing else would do.

In the midst of her fit, the phone rang. She looked at it, and so did Sheila. Then they looked up at each other.

"Oh my God!" Naomi screamed. "You think it's him?"

Sheila shrugged. She thought for certain things were over between the two of them. For him not to call for two whole weeks, Sheila was certain this lopsided relationship that had all but consumed Naomi was finally over.

Naomi grabbed the phone and pulled it up to her ear.

"H-h-hello?"

"Hi, how are you?"

"Oh my God!"

"Can I send the car for you?"

"Yes!"

"How much time will you need?"

"Thirty minutes. I'll be ready."

"I'll see you shortly, then."

When she hung up the phone, Naomi turned to Sheila, and for the first time in days there was a smile on her face.

"I take it that was him," Sheila said.

Naomi instantly noticed the change in her demeanor, but she didn't give a damn.

"Yes, and I'm going to meet him. He's sending the car over." Naomi didn't wait for Sheila's response. She simply rushed into her bedroom and started to change clothes.

"So, you're just gonna run off and leave after you were just complaining that he hadn't called?"

"Umm-hmm."

"So you're just gonna jump up and run to his side because he called. What about what we talked about?"

Naomi emerged from her room as a new woman. She was smartly dressed in a pair of tailored pin-striped slacks and a crisp white shirt. The outfit gave her a smart and sophisticated look. She didn't want to hear a damn thing Sheila was talking about. All she knew was that she needed to see the senator with her own two eyes and find out what the hell she had done wrong.

But by the time she came face-to-face with the senator, her desire to find out what had happened had fallen so low on her priority list, she didn't even bring it up.

She strolled into the suite and smiled at the senator. "You look even better than I remember. I guess what they say is true, absence makes the heart grow fonder."

The senator acknowledged her presence, but something was different and Naomi sensed it right away.

"I missed your loving, your touch, your handsome face, I just missed you so much." Naomi removed her shirt. "How are you? How've you been?"

"I'm good."

"I'm glad to hear that." Naomi smiled again. What she really wanted to know was why he had gone missing in action for the past couple of weeks, but something told her not to bring it up until he did. For now, she just wanted to enjoy the pleasure of his company.

Naomi extended both hands to him. For a few seconds, he didn't move, just watched her. Then he accepted her hands and allowed her to pull him up. She led him up the stairs and into the bathroom.

In there, she helped him undress. She turned on the shower and stripped off the rest of her own clothes. Once they were both naked, she led him into the shower and washed his body carefully. The senator allowed her to have her way with him.

For the last two weeks he too had been living in hell. Beverly had signed them up for an Alaskan cruise with three other couples, and he was disgusted. He didn't enjoy himself at all. He thought continuously about Naomi and what she was doing.

"You cannot use the phone, BlackBerry, or computer, we need this time together," Beverly had said.

By day two the senator was ready to charter a plane and go to Naomi, but he resisted the urge. His mind was still working on what to do about Sheila.

The moment he held Naomi's nipples in between his forefinger and thumb he knew he was home. He remembered the look on her face when she strolled into the suite. She wasn't embarrassed to let him know that she had missed him terribly.

"Would you like dinner?"

"No, I want to give you some head."

He cracked a smile. The senator took Naomi's head between her hands and pulled it into his face. He kissed her hard and long. The kiss told her everything she'd wondered about.

When the kiss was over, he allowed her to get down on her knees and make good on her promise to give him head.

At first she handled him rough, tugging and pulling on his member. She bit and gnawed at it, then felt him swell in her mouth. Naomi kept her pierced stare on him as she worked. When he winced, she grabbed him and squeezed harder.

He released a strained moan, closed his eyes like he was savoring the sensation, and clutched her head.

Naomi worked at a frenzied pace, sucking and slurping and sucking. She was getting all wet, thinking about how he was feeling. She wanted him to feel fantastic.

He was stiff as steel when he finally moved her away. She turned in an attempt to move away, but he grabbed her and held her down. Naomi wasn't fighting him, but she felt odd.

The senator yanked off her clothes and shoved himself into her. He humped her like an animal and clutched her neck to hold her in place.

"Oh God! Oh God, Calvin! Oh God!"

12

Big Jim was waiting for his boss in the Houston office when he strode in with a smile of satisfaction still on his face. Big Jim was very familiar with that look, but he wasn't saying a word about it. He was just glad to know that he had done his job to his boss's satisfaction. The senator was generous when he was pleased.

The senator took a seat behind his desk and turned to Jim. "Lock the door."

"Oh yeah, this came for you," the giant of a man said as he moved to give the senator an envelope. Then he walked over and locked the door.

"It's the information on the other one," Jim said.

The senator smiled. "Good job, my man. I knew you could do it. Good job."

The envelope contained information about Sheila, most of the things you'd find by searching for someone online. It contained her address, phone number, current place of employment, date of birth, and whether she owned any property in Harris County. But that information was least of interest to the senator. He flipped through the pages until he found what he was looking for.

"Everybody's got a secret, Big Jim." He plucked a few pictures from the stack of information, and a smile came to his face.

"Yes, boss, we've all got 'em, that's for sure." Jim scrutinized the pictures the senator slid over to him. He snickered briefly as he looked at each one.

Senator Davis knew he had to figure out Sheila's agenda, and he needed to do it before things got out of hand. From her credit report he could see she was up to her ears in debt, barely living paycheck to paycheck. Her track record in the dating department indicated she hopped from man to man at leisure. But it appeared she wasn't seeing anyone at the time.

"Why is she so interested in Naomi?" Nothing in the paperwork indicated any way Sheila could benefit from knowing about his relationship with Naomi, or at least nothing he could see right away.

"You want me to have someone watch her? I could get a tail on her within the hour," Big Jim informed Senator Davis.

The senator shook his head. "Nah, not yet. Not just yet, I think we need to wait and see what happens. Maybe drop some important information through Naomi and see how fast it travels and where it lands. For all I know, it's probably just two women gossiping. You know how they are."

Big Jim shook his head. "That's all they do!" He and the senator broke into laughter.

"I think for now, Naomi probably just needed someone to talk to. We'll see if she picked the wrong person."

"So we're just gonna let them keep yapping back and forth like that?"

"Well, right now it looks like Naomi just complains about little things here and there. I don't know that it's anything to worry about."

"So we do nothing?" Jim shrugged his massive shoulders.

"I'll keep an eye on 'em." The senator flipped through the folder again. He stopped when something else caught his eye. A devilish grin spread across his face. "Shame, shame, shame."

No, Sheila wouldn't be a problem for him and Naomi, no way, no how. If she knew what was best for her, she'd make sure she listened to Naomi's complaints, and keep her opinions to herself.

If it appeared Sheila was going to interfere, the senator figured he'd simply have to send her a message.

The senator started reading more about Sheila's little secret. One he was certain she wouldn't want anyone to know about. His eyebrows elevated, nearly to his hairline. He shook his head and decided Sheila was of no real threat to his relationship at all. And if he turned out to be wrong, the contents of the envelope were certainly enough to destroy her if he had to.

13

Naomi felt like one of her many students who had gotten a case of spring fever. In class, she often sat around daydreaming about where she'd rather be. She had seen the senator just about every weekend for the last three months. It was so hard to believe that in a few days they would've been together for eight months. They had met in October right before the election and already she felt like a permanent fixture in his life.

When he wasn't able to make it for whatever reason, he would call to let her know. When he couldn't call, he'd find a way to get word to her. Despite the fact that the senator had proven himself to Naomi, Sheila still disapproved of the way Naomi was handling the relationship.

"You shouldn't have sex with him every time you're together."

"Why not?"

"Because he'll grow tired of you."

For a while, Naomi would listen, actually placing stock in what Sheila was saying. But the moment she'd see the senator, all of Sheila's advice would go out the window.

It was almost like a cycle. Naomi would discuss the details of her wonderful weekend with the senator, and Sheila would find something wrong with some aspect of it.

"I can't believe you have anal sex with him." Sheila shook her head in disgust.

"I happen to enjoy it and so does he, so what's the big deal?"

Sheila sucked her teeth. "Girl, he'll never leave his wife for you. You don't know how to play the game."

Despite her attempt to ignore the negativity, Naomi couldn't help herself. If she didn't know how to play the game, why was her relationship with the senator stronger than ever? They'd been on so many weekend getaway trips, he'd given her fine lingere, nice jewelry, and even bought her a new car, but still Sheila found problems with the relationship.

"You shouldn't let him buy you all those things," she once said.

"And why not?"

Sheila would shake her head. "Because you don't want him to think you're just in it for what you can get."

Naomi thought about that and she figured Sheila was right to a certain point. She wasn't with the senator for the gifts and trips, but she enjoyed them. She wondered if he thought she was a gold digger. There was a constant fight brewing in Naomi's head when it came to her relationship with the senator.

On one shoulder stood Sheila wielding her unsolicited advice; on the other was the senator. Then there was the fact that she had fallen in love. Sheila had hit the roof when Naomi admitted it.

They were on the patio having lunch at Papadouxs off Kirby yesterday evening.

"What's wrong with you?" Sheila asked.

"I've got a problem."

Sheila's eyes widened. She leaned in after looking around to make sure no one they recognized was there.

"What kind of problem?" Her face was contorted into a frown.

Naomi stabbed at her salad with her fork.

"Girrrl, what is it? Syphilis, Gonorrhea? Hmmm, I've had them all," she whispered.

Naomi frowned and looked up at Sheila. "Girl! I'm not talking about no doggone disease!" She lowered her head when she noticed a few other customers looking toward their table.

"Um, I think I'm in love with the senator."

"What?" Sheila screamed. "Are you crazy? I would've rather you were harboring an STD. How could you! We talked about this!" She shook her head in disgust. Sheila was too through with Naomi. How could she have been so careless and stupid? They'd talked about this time and time again.

Naomi felt like a disobedient teenager under her mother's scrutiny. "I couldn't help it. He's so good to me. I mean, he takes such good care of me, I've never had a man treat me this way before."

Sheila sighed. She twirled her straw in her glass and decided she needed to handle her friend delicately. Naomi was still the same naive woman-child who had lucked up on a powerful man nearly a year ago and didn't know what to do with him.

"Well, I guess it's not so bad. I mean, in all honesty, I didn't think you guys would make it this long. Do you think he feels the same way about you?"

Naomi shrugged. She wasn't sure. She really didn't even care. She just knew she loved the senator and that was all that mattered.

"We can fix this, you know," Sheila said after a few minutes of silence.

"Fix what? You act like I've got some disease that penicillin will cure. I don't want to be fixed. I'm in love. That's nothing to be gloomy about."

Sheila looked around the courtyard again and leaned in. "Normally you'd be a hundred percent correct, but the problem with this love affair is he's a very married senator. And I doubt he would walk out on his family for you. That would be the end of his career. Remember, this is someone who was elected to office on a very moral platform."

Naomi knew every word Sheila was saying was true. She wasn't proud of the fact that she had fallen in love with him either, but there was very little she could do about it.

"See, if you'd been seeing someone else like I told you to, you wouldn't be in this situation now."

"No, you're right, I wouldn't be, I would just be a big ol' nasty ho!"

"Girl, don't knock the hos 'cause they know how to keep it strictly business. Trust when I say they don't go falling in love with the tricks, it's strictly business. See, that's how you shoulda handled the senator. No strings attached, no catching feelings, just hit it, and get paid!" Sheila clapped her hands. "Bam! Nobody gets hurt!"

Naomi didn't even bother to respond. She finished

her lunch and daydreamed about how perfect her life would be if the senator decided to leave his family for her.

She knew it was a long shot, but still she could dream. Then suddenly she looked up at Sheila. "What if he did leave them to be with me?"

Sheila dropped her fork. "Girl, don't start no shit!" she warned.

"No, I'm serious. Why shouldn't we be together? We love each other. Why would he want to stay with that ol' hag?"

"Look, I'm telling you, get those thoughts out of your head right now! If you know what's best for you, you'll go out and get yourself something on the side and keep it cute as far as the senator is concerned. Mark my words, that's the best move for you at this point."

Naomi didn't care what Sheila was talking about. She was determined to beat the odds. And when she was done, she'd be the new Mrs. Calvin Davis, wife of the still prominent state senator.

14

Senator Davis had long suspected things had changed between him and Naomi. He felt it too, and at times he wanted to do nothing more than throw caution to the wind. He deserved to be happy just like everyone else. But he also realized he had far too much to lose. When he was alone at times, he'd envision life as a simple man, a poor man, and the thought brought sheer terror to his heart. That was a risk he could not bear to take.

Beverly had come from a prominent family of doctors. She was accustomed to living a certain lifestyle and he had been able to provide her with that, but now he was tired. He was tired of her attitude that said she deserved everything he worked so hard for and more.

Life with Naomi would be very different, simple even. But he couldn't leave his children; it would ruin their lives and he couldn't sleep at night knowing he had done that. If Beverly filed for divorce, she'd take him to the cleaners, that much he knew for certain. The headlines would be enough to bring his promising career to a screeching halt.

He eased back in his leather chair and closed his eyes. He allowed his mind to escape to thoughts of Naomi working her magic on him.

"Come on, Daddy," she'd coo.

It turned him on, made him feel young again. Naomi was good for him and he couldn't remember a time when he'd felt so happy and free.

"Take it all, Daddy, it's all yours."

She hadn't been well traveled until they met. Every place he took her was thrilling, new, and exciting, and she'd fuck his brains out to show her appreciation. Naomi loved it when he filled her up, she didn't care how she got it, and she was so insatiable. Each morning he woke her up by filling her with his juices. When he didn't wake her that way, she'd pout and threaten a grumpy day until he gave her what she wanted. She loved sex and loved giving it to him any way he wanted it.

Senator Davis turned to the monitor of Naomi's apartment. She was walking from the bedroom to the kitchen. She was wearing a dainty little camisole and he felt himself begin to expand. He couldn't get enough of her no matter how much he tried. She was like an addictive drug.

As Naomi stood at the kitchen counter drinking a glass of water, he wished for a zoom mechanism on the camera. Something didn't seem right about her expression, as if she was troubled about something. He wanted to reach out to her and ease all of her worries. He wanted to do more for her, as much as he possibly could. He wasn't set to visit with her the upcoming weekend because of his daughter's birthday party, but oh how he wanted to.

When he grew tired of teasing himself by watching her, he flicked off the monitor and turned to the view from his window.

A knock at the door broke his solitude.

"Yes!"

Matt stuck his head into the office. "Senator, here's something we thought you might like to read."

Senator Davis nodded slightly.

Matt walked into the office. He was carrying a newspaper in his hand. "I don't think it's really a big deal, but we just like to stay on top of stuff like this, you know, so we're always prepared."

The newspaper article was circled in red. It was about a conservative radio talk show host who announced he would run for office the following year. Senator Davis was amused by the article. He wasn't ready to give up his seat, and when he did he was going to Washington, but not because he lost out to some conservative shock jock. His eyes glanced over the article; the man was touting the inevitable end to the traditional family and discussing everything he'd do to reinstate morality into marriage.

Matt stood in front of his desk as he browsed the article.

"Thanks."

"Should I file it?"

"No, not necessary. Tell Vanessa to book me a speaking engagement in Houston for this weekend."

Matt didn't move right away. He looked at the senator as if he didn't really understand.

"Wh-what kind of engagement?" he stammered.

"Figure something out!" The senator hated when

he had to raise his voice, but at times he wondered what his aides were thinking.

He got up from his desk and walked down the hall to another senator's office.

"Bob, you free for lunch?"

"Hey, Calvin. Sure, let me wrap up something and I'll be right there."

Senator Davis turned to leave, but the other senator motioned for him to wait.

"I'll only be a second. No need to go off."

Senator Davis figured he'd spend a couple of hours catching up on the latest gossip floating around the capitol. He hoped that would be enough to take his mind off his tender little young thing. So far nothing else had worked.

15

Naomi was tired of the way things were going in her relationship with the senator. If he really didn't love Beverly, why couldn't he be with her? She'd decided to put her foot down and let him know exactly where she stood on the matter.

But before she could make her demands known, she suffered a blow of her own.

"Yes, you are approximately seven weeks pregnant. Congratulations!" the doctor cheered. Naomi's head began to spin. Pregnant? What would the senator do or say when he found out?

It had been two days since she got the news, and all she could do was replay the doctor's words in her head over and over again.

"Yes, you are approximately seven weeks pregnant. Congratulations!"

She had gotten pregnant. How could she have allowed that to happen?

She also remembered the sound of the senator's voice when he called to tell her he had a speaking engagement in Houston and he needed her at the suite by six Friday evening.

"I have something I need to discuss with you," she had said.

"We can talk about anything you want. Friday at six." Then the line went dead.

Normally the days leading up to her visit with the senator seemed to drag by slowly. This time, however, Friday came faster than she wanted or needed. She hadn't decided what she was gonna say.

Walking into the suite that doubled as their love nest was more difficult than she had ever imagined it could be.

The senator was upstairs; she could hear his footsteps. She took the laborious walk up the winding stairs and dropped her bag at her feet.

"I didn't hear you come in."

She offered him a faint smile.

The senator kissed her hard and long. She tried not to give in, but her heart wouldn't allow it. She buckled under the pressure and soon they were stripping each other's clothes off.

News of the pregnancy could wait. She needed his touch, wanted desperately to feel him inside her.

"I want you on top, so I can look into your eyes. I've missed you."

"Whatever you want, Daddy, whatever you want."

Their bodies became one and danced to a sensual rhythm. Naomi knew this was right, they were right; he had to leave Beverly, he just had to. Once the senator learned she was pregnant, he'd do the right thing, he'd make sure they were a family.

As they lay in the afterglow of sex, Naomi snuggled next to the senator and took a deep breath. "Calvin?"

"Yes, baby? You ready for another round?" He chuckled; he loved her sexual appetite.

"Um, not just yet, unless you are."

"I need a few minutes, and I'll be ready to go again."

"Well, I wanted to ask you something. How do you feel about having more children?" Naomi closed her eyes as she waited for his answer. She felt his chest move up, then down.

"More kids? Baby, I already took care of that. I'm done in that department."

"What do you mean?"

"Oh, I got a vasectomy a few years ago," he said.

Naomi's head began to spin. Her throat got dry and she felt her eyes filling with tears.

"You did what?" Naomi was bewildered. How could that be possible? The doctor said she was seven weeks pregnant.

"Yep, Beverly and I have our hands full with two, didn't want any more. Why do you ask?"

"Oh, no reason, just curious," Naomi said sadly.

The senator leaned up and looked down.

"Uh-oh, looks like something's ready for round two." He smiled.

Naomi thought she was gonna puke.

16

Naomi sat at her desk during her conference period with a blank look on her face. She barely wanted to be alive, much less at work, today. Sheila had called out to her twice, but still she didn't respond.

"Girl, what's wrong wit' you?"

"I'm pregnant."

Sheila flopped down on a nearby chair. She stared off into space as well. "Okay, so what did the senator say about this? I should've seen this coming."

"It's not his."

Sheila's head snapped in her direction.

"What? You been seeing someone else?" Sheila balked. Was there more to Naomi than she realized? Could her innocent exterior have been an act all along?

"The senator is the only man I've been with in the last two years."

Sheila shook her head. "I don't understand."

When Naomi turned to face Sheila, tears spilled from her eyes and down her cheeks. She shook her own head. Soon her sobs turned to a gut-wrenching howl. Sheila rushed to her side to offer comfort.

"It's gonna be okay. It's gonna be okay."

After crying on Sheila's shoulders for a few minutes, Naomi looked up and said, "I'm so confused. I've taken a hundred pregnancy tests and the results are all the same. The doctors took a blood test, but it doesn't make sense," she sobbed.

"Okay, calm down, just calm down," Sheila encouraged. "You've gotta stay calm."

When Naomi's door swung open, both their eyes widened in horror.

"What's going on in here?"

They looked into Diane's unforgiving stare.

"We're on conference," Sheila quickly responded.

"Yeah, but why is this one in tears?"

"It's personal."

Naomi continued to cry. It didn't make sense and she didn't know what to make of it.

"You know, lately there's been quite a bit going on with the two of you. I need you to keep your personal lives at home and not here at work." Spittle gathered at the corners of Diane's mouth. The women didn't know why she was such a bitter old woman.

She slammed the door shut behind her. Naomi looked at Sheila with red puffy eyes. "I just don't understand how this could be."

"I know, I know. Look, why don't we get through the day here at work? Then we'll grab some takeout and go to your house."

Students in Naomi's classes did whatever they felt like and she did very little to stop them. Her mind was elsewhere and she found it difficult to concentrate on anything.

On her way back to her own classroom, Sheila ducked into one of the janitor's closets. She pulled out her cell phone and dialed a number.

"Hey, didn't I tell you this day would come?" She struggled to talk on the phone while listening for anyone who might be coming. "I'll have more details for you later. I need to run."

She heard footsteps. "Look, I've gotta go, I'll call you when I have more information. Just get ready to make a move."

When the janitor opened the door and saw Sheila inside, she frowned.

"Oh, I was looking for some bleach," she lied.

The janitor wasn't buying her lie. She looked at Sheila skeptically, then sucked her teeth.

"Hope you found what you wanted. The bleach," the janitor snarled.

"Umph." Sheila rolled her eyes, then stepped out of the closet and moved down the hall toward her classroom. She walked with her head held high, higher than she'd been able to do in a long time.

"Cha-ching!" she muttered to herself. "Finally, I've hit the jackpot!"

Sheila could hardly wait for the final bell to ring. She couldn't wait to get to Naomi's apartment and get the business. She plucked her cell phone from her purse and pushed a number to speed-dial her friend. "Naomi, you okay?"

"No, I'm not."

"You on your way home?"

"I'm already here. I left early."

"What? What did Diane say?"

"I really don't care. I just left, I wasn't feeling well, so I left."

Sheila's heart was pounding so loudly she felt it in her ears. This girl was truly messed up, she didn't realize to what extent.

"Okay, well, I'm gonna stop at Taco Cabana and pick up some food for us. Just hang in there, I'll be there in about twenty minutes."

"Don't get any food for me, I don't wanna eat."

"Look, you're eating for two now, you can't act like that. I'll be there shortly, okay?"

"Okay."

Sheila stopped at the restaurant and arrived at Naomi's apartment in record time. She brought enough food to feed a small army.

When Naomi opened her front door, she was a complete wreck, worse off than Sheila remembered from earlier. Sheila wanted to know everything, but she didn't want to push her too much too soon.

She carefully placed the food on top of the breakfast island in Naomi's kitchen and pulled two paper plates from a cabinet.

Once each plate was stacked with a variety of food, she took them both to the living room and placed them on the coffee table.

At first Sheila ate alone and in silence. Naomi didn't look at her or the food, she just stared off into space. She'd go from stone faced to sobbing in a matter of seconds. Then she'd go back to staring off again.

"Okay, now tell me what happened."

Naomi shrugged. "It's simple, I'm pregnant. I went to the doctor and she told me I was seven weeks pregnant. I waited to tell the senator until I saw him face-to-face."

"Well, what did he say when you told him? How did he react?"

"He didn't answer right away." Naomi shook her head. "Well, I didn't really get to tell him."

"Why not?"

"Well, because I asked him if he wanted more children. I wanted to see what he would say."

"What did he say?"

"He said he couldn't because he had already had a vasectomy to make sure he didn't."

Sheila's eyes grew wide. She put down the piece of quesadilla she was eating, then looked up at Naomi.

"Naomi, don't you see what's going on here? He knows you're pregnant, that's why he said that. He knows damn well he's fucked up! Girl, stop crying. You're pregnant, he knows it's his and now he's panicking. That's all this is."

For the first time since she was devastated by the senator's reaction, Naomi thought she may have found some hope. She didn't even consider that. Could the senator have only been reacting out of fear?

She sniffled and looked at Sheila.

"You sure you haven't been sleeping with anyone else?"

"No, I swear, I swear, he's the only one. You know how I feel about him."

Sheila nodded. "Okay, let me tell you what we need to do next."

17

Sheila couldn't wait to leave Naomi's house and her issues. She finally felt like she was making strides. The moment she arrived outside, she pulled out her cell and dialed a number.

"I'm on my way," she said, then ended the call.

Her heart was threatening to leap from her chest even before he pulled his front door open. Only moments before, Sheila had stood petrified, wondering how this would all work out. Sure, she had information, but the thought of being with him was exhilarating. Sheila had agreed to his request and considered backing out several times, but didn't, and this time she was ready to do whatever he wanted.

When the door swung open, she pulled her jacket open, smiled, and hoped he couldn't sense her apprehension. She had gone the extra mile for men in the past, but this was a bit over the top and she knew it.

At first, he just stood there, and Sheila felt a bit uneasy. The door was open long enough for the evening breeze to hit her bare breasts. In that instant, she followed his stare right down to her breasts, and stuck her chest out a bit more.

"What took you so long?" he asked, with his eyes still on her chest.

"I couldn't just up and leave her after what she just told me. I had to play it cool for a moment," she said, using the sexiest voice she could muster up. He glanced around a bit, giving Sheila even more reason to worry. But things started looking up real soon.

"So we're good to go, then?"

"Man! You don't know the half of it!" Sheila confirmed.

He offered a devilish grin. Her nipples were rock hard, and standing at full attention. Sheila licked her lips, then smiled real slow and easy before licking them again. He finally moved aside to let her in.

"I really am sorry I'm late," she said in that husky voice she knew he liked so much. "So, what do you have planned for me this evening?"

"Well, how about we get to business first? Let me hear what you've got for me." He cleared his throat. The truth was, although Sheila was originally in this for the money, she had started feeling uncomfortable because most times he made it clear he only wanted information. And sometimes it appeared as if he wanted information more than he wanted her.

"I was thinking we could do some other things first, then get to the business, if you know what I mean." Sheila slowly reached up and squeezed her breasts. She released a seductive moan as her fingers gripped and released her flesh.

From what Sheila could see, he was damn near drooling at the mouth, but she honestly didn't know if his lust was for the information or her.

Sheila reached down and stroked the area between her thighs. "I think I'm getting wetter by the minute, but I guess I'll just have to figure out what to do about my little problem, huh?"

The moment he had opened the front door, Sheila made sure her entire upper body was exposed.

"I don't like to be kept waiting. You know how I feel about punctuality," he said sternly.

Sheila knew how he felt about such little things. Actually just about every little thing that was either out of place, or seemed like it might be, irritated him, but she also knew how badly he wanted the information.

Without any warning or changes in his cold demeanor he pulled Sheila into his arms. The kiss she was expecting never came. He looked into her eyes and said, "You'd better not be bullshittin' me!"

Sheila didn't respond right away. She tried to ignore the shiver of fear she felt and hoped to change his mind with the lure of available sex.

When he turned and strolled into the room, she was hot on his heels. He pulled his stiff member from his pants and Sheila was on it before he could fully free himself.

Despite his struggle to maintain his hard-core image, he couldn't deny the magic she was working with her mouth. Soon he just grabbed the back of her head and held on for the ride.

At some point during the rendezvous, they had moved to the massive bed. They had wrestled there for a good forty-five minutes when he grabbed her by the throat and pulled himself out of her to release his juices on her breasts.

When they collapsed next to each other on the

bed, Sheila knew better than to attempt to snuggle. He didn't play that shit, not even a little bit. Despite his emotional detachment, she lay spent and completely satisfied. When he disappeared into the bathroom, she just turned over and yawned. She had no reason to think the sound of an opening door was anyone but him.

"You must be Sheila," a soft voice said, startling her nearly to death. Sheila bolted up in bed and scrambled to cover her bare breasts. She turned to see a woman dressed in a small negligee with fishnet stockings and stacked heels.

"Uh, hi," Sheila said, swallowing dryly.

"Didn't mean to scare you," the woman said, and made her way to the foot of the bed. In the throes of passion, Sheila had forgotten all about their little agreement.

"I'm Jewels," the woman said. Soon she stepped up on the bed, with her heels still on, and started gyrating around one of the four massive bedposts. Sheila's eyes were fixed on her as she lowered herself in a sensual dance move. Sheila's brain kept telling her she wasn't attracted to women, but Jewels had her second-guessing herself and the facts. Sheila could see the line of her wetness in the crotch of the thong. She swiped at it, giggled, and said, "See, your little fine ass got me dripping wet."

Was that a compliment? Sheila wondered. She wasn't quite sure what to do, so she just sat there nervously praying he would hurry up. Despite her brain's reminder regarding her sexual preference, she felt a warm pool settling between her own thighs and her nipples were once again hard.

"I see you've met Jewels," he said, smiling as

Jewels stood now rubbing on her fully naked body. Jewels was a thick, five-foot-six, caramel-brown color with clear and shiny skin. She had already established that she was ready to do whatever, when he walked over and started caressing her body.

"Sheila, lie back and open your legs," he commanded, without even taking his eyes off Jewels and her sensual dance. She hesitated a bit but did as she was told.

Sheila figured this, along with the information she had, would definitely change her standing.

18

Hours after he had witnessed the drama playing out in Naomi's living room, Senator Davis was still fired up. "What the fuck is she trying to do to me?" he yelled at the screen. He couldn't fathom the situation he now found himself in. He watched the situation from the moment Sheila arrived at the apartment. And he was pissed from the moment the two started talking.

"Naomi, don't you see what's going on here? He knows you're pregnant, that's why he said that. He knows damn well he's fucked up! Girl, stop crying. You're pregnant, he knows it's his, and now he's panicking. That's all this is."

He had long ago yearned for the early days of his relationship with Naomi. Those days when what they had was sweet and a refreshing relief, when she was so thrilled to be with him. Then suddenly she started talking to her friend and ever since then things had been going downhill.

Senator Davis was planning to tell her not to keep the baby, that there was just no way she could keep it. But when Naomi asked him about children, he did panic; he didn't know what to do. He didn't know what to say. He could tell something was different about her; he had seen the worried expression on her face as he peeked in on her from his office.

Senator Davis knew he should've enlisted Big Jim's help long ago, he shouldn't have allowed this mess to go on like this, but the truth was he couldn't imagine Naomi ever doing anything to cause him harm. He knew she loved him, and he knew she'd never leave. But he didn't expect this turn of events. Now he was in a position he didn't like being in: on the defensive, reacting.

He picked up his BlackBerry and dialed Big Jim. "Where are you?"

"I can be there in five minutes."

"Good. We have a problem."

Before he hung up, Senator Davis could hear tires screeching. He loved Jim's loyalty and dedication. If anyone could get him out of this mess, he knew it would be Jim. He almost breathed a sigh of relief at the thought of being able to turn to someone close for help. Jim would take his secrets to the grave, clutching them tightly with his cold hands before revealing a thing about his boss.

Four minutes later, Big Jim came bursting through the senator's office door. He was breathing hard and heavy. "Whassup, boss?" His dark eyes scanned the room, he was ready to take the necessary action.

"We've got a problem brewing in Houston."

Big Jim leaned over the senator's desk. "Lemme guess. It's our friend, she's stirring shit up?"

"Yeah. There's a baby involved. I don't like the direction this conversation has taken."

Big Jim looked at the two women hugging on the screen. He knew it must be serious if the senator looked as spooked as he did. "You think she's up to something?"

"I think it's gonna be hard to isolate her and make her do the right thing with this one constantly in her ear."

"Hmmm."

"We need to find out who, if anyone, she's talking to. How difficult do you think it would be for your people to get into her place?"

"We can get into any place, hers included."

"Okay, let's make it happen."

They watched and listened to the rest of the conversation between Naomi and Sheila. Sheila told Naomi what she had was valuable, that most women would give a right arm to be in her position.

"Crying is the last thing you should be doing. Don't you understand? You now hold the trump card. That little baby is your ticket to whatever the hell you want."

Naomi didn't respond. But a few minutes later, when she got up and walked to the bathroom, the senator and Big Jim watched as Sheila twisted her head to make sure the bathroom door was closed completely.

Sheila jumped up from the couch and grabbed her bag. She looked around the room like she was about to do something she didn't want anyone to see; then she dug into her purse and pulled out a small recorder.

"What the fuck?" the senator screeched.

They watched as she checked the device, shook

it, and pressed a few buttons. She held it up to her ear, then rushed and put it back in her purse.

Sheila moved the purse closer to where Naomi was sitting, then waited for her so-called friend to return from the bathroom.

"Okay, let's go over this again. I need time to think. Tell me again what Senator Davis said when you told him you were pregnant with his baby. I need to know everything, and don't leave anything out. The smallest detail might give us a clue about what he's trying to do."

The senator and Big Jim looked at each other.

"What the fuck is this bitch up to?"

"I dunno, boss, but I'm damn sure gonna find out."

19

Naomi didn't know what to do. She rolled Sheila's suggestion around in her head several times and it just didn't feel right. Another thing that just didn't feel right was the fact that the senator was not returning any of her calls.

How could their relationship have turned sour so fast? She still yearned for him late at night. She still woke in cold sweats dreaming of being with him. This was no way to live and she knew it. For the sake of their baby, she had to fix things with the senator, and she had to fix them fast.

Once again she picked up her phone and dialed the senator.

To her astonishment, this time he answered on the second ring.

"Senator Davis here."

"Calvin?"

Silence.

Five beats later he finally spoke again.

"Yes."

"Oh, baby, what's wrong? Why aren't you returning

my calls? You don't even call me anymore. I have to
see you, I need to see you right away," she pressed.

Senator Davis didn't say anything.

"Are you still there? Did you hang up?"

"My schedule is pretty tight."

"I know, but maybe I could come to Austin so we
could talk in person. I really need to talk to you."

"What is it, Naomi? What's so urgent?"

"Not like this, not over the phone. I need to see
you. And I know you need to see me too."

She was hoping her place in his heart was still
there. She wanted to be in his arms; she knew that
was the only way she could convince him that they
could, should, be a family.

"I need to run."

"Please, Calvin, don't do this to me. Please, I
really need to talk to you, I need to see you."

The next thing Naomi heard was the dial tone
ringing in her ear. Her heart dropped. Could it really
be over? Did he just hang up in her face like that?
She inspected her phone, hoping something had
gone wrong with the line. The truth was far too dev-
astating for her to accept.

Was Sheila right? That she really did have the
trump card? Was she gonna have to play hardball
with the senator? She shook the thoughts from her
head. Naomi tucked her feet beneath her butt as she
sat on her sofa wondering what she should do next.

Nothing made sense. She felt stupid, like some
teen who'd gone and gotten herself knocked up by
some irresponsible kid. But Senator Davis was far
from a kid, he was only one of the most influential
men in the state of Texas.

"He knows damn well he's fucked up! Girl, stop

crying. You're pregnant, he knows it's his, and now he's panicking. That's all this is."

Sheila's words rang out in her head. But still, she was confused; she didn't know what to do.

"Crying is the last thing you should be doing." Naomi tried to believe that, but it was hard. She was convinced; Sheila was looking at a completely different situation.

"Don't you understand? You now hold the trump card." She didn't feel the least bit powerful. What good was a damn trump card if your man didn't want to be bothered anyway?

"That little baby is your ticket to whatever the hell you want." But what happened if the senator himself was all she wanted? She didn't want money from him, she didn't want to ruin his life or his career, she only wanted them to be together as a family, why couldn't he see that?

Naomi couldn't bear the thought of losing him. He had been everything to her; her life truly began once they were together. She just wanted things to go back to the way they had been.

Why couldn't the senator understand they could have great days all the time, not just during those stolen moments? All he had to do was leave Beverly and his kids. Hell, he could even bring the kids. Naomi loved kids. She had to see him face-to-face. If she did, she knew she could win him over.

Three weeks had gone by and still no call from the senator. She was a wreck, a pregnant wreck. Occasionally, Sheila would come over to check her progress, but even that had become a challenge.

Sheila was always bombarding her with a ton of questions. Has the senator called yet? What happens when he calls you? What are you gonna do? Is our plan still the way you want to go?

Naomi didn't want to think about Sheila's stupid-ass plan. She wasn't trying to push the senator further away; her hope was to win him back.

After pacing the living room, then the bedroom for nearly an hour, Naomi decided she was gonna take action. She tried to call and run her own idea by Sheila, but she didn't answer her phone.

Naomi ate dinner, then took a long, hot bath and retired to bed. She had a huge day ahead of her, and it had been a while since she took a road trip.

20

"What the fuck!" Sheila hollered. This was the first time she'd brought a man back to her place in months, and although it wasn't a date or anything like that, she couldn't help but feel warm with embarrassment.

"Damn, looks like a tornado swept through this place," David commented.

They both took careful steps trying to sidestep anything that might be salvageable. Sheila kept looking around as her blood began to boil. She couldn't believe this foolishness. The more she walked through her apartment, the more upset she became. Everything was a wreck. Just like David said, it appeared as if a tornado had blown through, leaving nothing but debris in its wake.

"Someone was really searching for something!" David said again. Her sofa, the love seat, the entertainment center were all tussled and turned over. Her books, magazines, pictures were strewn all over, helping to cover the mess.

"Damn, please tell me you saved the tapes

someplace other than here," David hissed. "There's shit all over the damn place." He looked around, taking in the mess.

Sheila's eyes grew wide. She shook her head. This had nothing to do with that; she was just a victim of random crime. Maybe a crackhead was looking for money and flipped out when there was none. She rushed into the bedroom and realized every room in her apartment was trashed. Clothes from the closets were thrown all over the floors. Sheila rushed to her nightstand, but before she even realized the drawers were out and emptied, she already knew it was gone!

"Damn!" She flopped onto a pile of clothes on the floor. "They took it," she said through clenched teeth. Now she was pissed.

"What?" David stood over her. "You didn't have any backups?" he asked, exasperated.

Sheila was hot. "Why would I have thought I needed backup?" She shook her head. There was no way she'd be able to recover even half the material she had on her digital recorder. This could not be happening to her. Not when she was so close to being debt free.

"So it's definitely gone, huh?"

She shrugged and nodded. "I know you don't believe me, right? You know, since I don't have the recordings? But the shit is true. I swear to you. You don't believe me, huh?"

"I didn't say that."

"Well, what should I do?" Sheila looked around at her apartment again. She was disgusted.

"Is there any way you can do it over again?" David asked hopefully.

"I suppose I'll have to, right?"

"You think you'll be able to?"

"Oh yeah, she likes to talk and basically I guess you can say I'm her confidante. I just need you guys to be patient with me."

"Look, we can be as patient as you need. Remember, we want what you've got, or what you had," David said as he once again looked around at the disaster.

Hours after David left, Sheila was still picking up the pieces of her life. She never realized just how much junk she had accumulated over the years. She had thought she had her stuff safely stashed, but obviously she didn't.

When the phone rang she dropped what she was holding. She knew if she didn't answer they'd keep calling. With horror in her eyes and fear in her heart, she walked over and picked up the phone. "Hello?"

There was silence on the other end.

Sheila turned and looked back over the mess in her living room. "I will have the fuckin' money, I just need a little more time."

She started trembling. She stood listening; then suddenly with shaky hands she put the phone back on its cradle. What was the point in standing there listening to someone breathe in her ear? The moment she turned her back the phone shrilled again. Tears were stinging in the corners of her eyes.

Tired of being harassed, she grabbed the receiver and barked, "I said I'll have your friggin' money!"

"Um, hello?" Naomi said softly.

"Oh, hey, Naomi, girl, I didn't know that was you."

"You okay, Sheila?"

"Yeah, girl, I'm fine."

"Who were you talking to? I mean, who you owe money to?"

"Oh, girl, it's nothing. You remember my ex, Bobby. I thought you was him, that's all."

"Well, I was calling to see if you wanted to come over, or we could go grab something to eat. I'm just feeling all messed up right now," Naomi said.

Sheila rolled her eyes. She didn't feel like baby-sitting her ass right now; she had her own damn problems. Then Naomi said something that instantly changed her mind.

"Besides, I finally talked to the senator."

"Oh?" Her ears perked up.

"Yeah, and, well, I guess I'm just feeling down about it."

"You know what? Have you eaten yet?"

"Nah, I've just been sitting here thinking about my conversation with the senator."

"Well, why don't I pick up some food and come on over? I'm a little bored anyway."

"I could order in if you don't feel like picking up something. You brought food last time."

"Yeah, but I don't mind."

"No, let me. You just come over and I'll call and have something delivered," Naomi persisted.

"All right, I'll be there in fifteen minutes. Let me pack a bag in case I decide to stay over."

Before she went to Naomi's Sheila stopped at Office Depot. She purchased a state-of-the-art digital voice recorder. It was similar to the old one she had, but she made sure this one had software-downloading capabilities.

Outside Naomi's front door, Sheila activated the record mechanism, then knocked. She straightened her clothes as she waited for Naomi to answer. Sheila patted her purse; she knew the recorder was working and this one was capable of recording eight full hours.

"Hey!" Naomi greeted her with a smile.

"Hey yourself!" Sheila walked in. She put her bag near the sofa, but placed her purse on the coffee table the moment she realized where Naomi had been sitting.

Naomi walked over to the coffee table. She glanced at Sheila's purse, then took her seat.

"The food should be here in about thirty minutes. I ordered Chinese. I hope that's fine."

"Girl, yes."

Naomi took a deep breath and placed her palms on top of her knees. She closed her eyes, then said, "It's over!"

Sheila's eyes grew wide. She felt her own heart racing. "What do you mean it's over?"

"The senator and me, it's over. He hung up on me earlier and when I tried to call back he didn't answer. He hasn't taken any of my calls since."

"Oh my God! What're you gonna do about the baby?"

Naomi shook her head as tears gushed down her face like Niagara Falls.

"Uh-huh. Oh no, you don't!" Sheila demanded. "You need to cut the tears right now. And I'm gonna tell you, we need to let the senator know, it won't be that easy to get rid of you!"

"But I don't wanna do anything to hurt him," Naomi whined. "I just don't want to make this any worse than it has to be. I'll be fine, I just need to start the process of getting over him."

"Girl, puh-leeease! This is now war! It's each woman for herself. The senator has already drawn the line. Now it's your move. And I'll be damned if I sit by while you suffer, just 'cause you're worried about protecting him." Sheila moved to the sofa to be next to Naomi.

"It's no longer about you, you've got a baby to think about. So stop all the damn crying and let's put our heads together on this thing."

Naomi appreciated Sheila's help, but she didn't have the courage to let her know about her own plan. It was just one of those things she felt she had to do alone. So far Sheila's advice had done nothing but left her lonely and in tears, and she was tired of being that way. Naomi decided it was finally time for her to take some action of her own, and she didn't feel like being talked out of it.

21

Senator Davis was wearing a permanent path in the plush carpet in his office. Everyone had gone home hours ago, and Beverly had called twice to remind him about a dinner party she planned. But his mind was elsewhere. He had really fucked up this time, there was no doubt about that at this point.

"So, this bitch has been recording details of my relationship with Naomi for months." His eyes glared at the mountain of evidence sitting on his desk. There was a small recorder with numerous minicassette tapes. The tapes were marked, logged by date and subject, in what seemed to be a well-thought-out filing system.

"I'm still working on the connection. It may take a minute, but I'm sure there's one."

"You should just handle this. Both of 'em," the senator said without flinching.

Big Jim held up his finger. His sidekick was present too. Usually he was the one who overreacted, quick to pull the trigger or quick to resort to violence. It was just his nature. But this time he was the only one in the room thinking with a level head. "Not yet, boss. There's no point in wiping them both out when we don't know who she's talking to. Let's just say she's working with the feds. She comes up missing, guess who they come visit?"

The senator rubbed his face. Jim was making sense; he had a good point. Senator Davis knew he had to listen to two of the best criminal minds he knew; it was why he hired them. But still, he was anxious. Each time they discussed what to do about Naomi and the snitch, Jim's nickname for Sheila, the senator approached the subject with mixed emotions. Yet his wife's words kept ringing out in his ears.

He really did care about Naomi. There was no question about that. She had gotten under his skin. At night he still dreamed of being between her silky thighs. He couldn't remember the last time he was attracted to such a submissive woman. He ruled everything while in her presence, and she truly appreciated his company. No woman had ever made him feel like so much of a man. He didn't have to be powerful with Naomi, he didn't have to make all of the right decisions. He was able to be himself. Now all of that was gone.

"So, how long will it take to figure out who she's working with?"

"We should have some information in a few days." Jim glanced at the two women on the screen. The three men had been watching since Sheila entered the apartment.

"Senator, maybe you should just bounce, go home, chill a bit. We'll put our heads together and figure out what to do until we get the information we need. Ain't no point in you sweating this. That's what you got us for, we can handle it."

Senator Davis looked at his guys with uncertainty. He knew there was nothing more he could do. But he also knew they needed the necessary information before they were able to move forward. "Well, I do have a dinner party to attend."

"Yeah, well, we'll drop you at the house. Then we'll talk more about how to handle this."

The ride home was long and quiet, giving the senator enough time to roll thoughts around in his head. Maybe he should've been excited when Naomi tried to tell him about the pregnancy. He knew it was his, she wasn't the type to run around, but he couldn't allow her to think they could just have a baby like newlyweds. He was married with children! Shit! He thought she understood the rules.

It wasn't really Naomi he was worried about, it was the advice she was getting from Sheila, who clearly had an agenda. He just needed to figure out what that agenda was all about.

The senator closed his eyes and leaned back in the bucket leather seat. He released a huge sigh. He knew he had to change his attitude before he stepped foot in the house. The last thing he needed was Beverly getting suspicious.

At times he couldn't begin to wrap his mind around the great potential for scandal that loomed over his head.

22

When Sheila and Naomi woke the next morning, they both dressed quickly and prepared to leave the house. At the door, Sheila turned to Naomi.

"We should just take your car so we could talk some more."

Naomi hesitated, her key still in the lock. "Um, I'm not going to work today." She pulled the key out and turned to walk down the hall.

"Wait!" Sheila yelled. "Where are you going? Why didn't you tell me?"

"Because I have some personal things to do, stuff I need to take care of." Naomi's eyes darted around the hall. She didn't want to tell Sheila any more than she had to because she didn't want to be talked out of it.

"Well, you have a doctor's appointment or something?"

"Uh-huh." Naomi nodded. It was just easier to have Sheila believe the lie. She didn't have time to sit and explain her plans, she just knew what she had to do and she was convinced she'd get no rest until she did.

The women went their separate ways. Sheila took Richmond and went toward downtown and Naomi took 610 to I-10 headed west. She got off at the beltway and hopped on 290 going west. Once she was on the outskirts of Houston, a sign indicated she was 142 miles from Austin.

Naomi settled in for the two-hour drive. She didn't quite know what she would say, but she was sick and tired of being sick and tired. She needed the senator to look her dead in the eye and tell her that she meant nothing to him, that the baby she was carrying, their baby meant nothing. Once he did that, she'd figure out her next move. But the point was, she didn't feel like sitting by idly, accepting brief phone calls with no explanation whatsoever.

She was determined; she'd made up her mind that he would have to deal with her personally. She wouldn't accept anything less.

By the time she pulled into the Austin city limits, she was tired, but still just as determined as she was when she had set out on the journey.

Naomi walked into the capitol and looked for the information desk. She was directed to the capitol secretary, who gave her directions to Senator Davis's office.

Thirty minutes later, she arrived at the senator's office. She pulled the door open. A receptionist was typing while talking into a headset. A tall, thin white man with unruly red hair walked out and looked like he jumped when he realized she was standing there.

"Uh, hi, is someone helping you?"

Naomi gave him her best smile and said, "No, actually, I was waiting for her to get off the phone."

"Oh, okay, I'm Matthew Branson, Senator Davis's assistant. Is there something I can help you with?"

Naomi tried to look around the office for signs of whether he was there. "I'm here to see Senator Davis. I drove in from Houston."

After she said it, she wished she could take it back. No one cared that she'd driven in from Houston. She stood quietly waiting for Matthew's response.

"Um, do you have an appointment? I mean, the senator is quite busy, he's on a conference call as we speak."

Naomi looked to the side and sat. "Well, as I said, I just drove in from Houston and I've got all day, so I'll just wait right here until he's done with his conference call."

Matt's eyebrows jumped up. He looked toward the senator's office, then back at Naomi. Something told him this might be one visitor the senator would not be eager to see, but he held his tongue. "What did you say your name was again?"

"Naomi Payne. He's not expecting me, but I'm positive he'll want to see me."

For a moment Matthew didn't move. He looked at Naomi with narrowed eyes. He sighed, then plucked a notepad from the desk.

"Naomi Payne," he said as he wrote her name.

Senator Davis's office was nothing like Naomi had imagined. The outer office was small and expertly decorated. There were several pieces of African art, three large paintings on separate walls, with a large HD plasma screen on another. The furniture consisted of a leather sofa and two matching suede wing chairs.

Large plants were in two corners of the room. A nice-smelling candle sat on an electric candle warmer.

While she sat waiting to see him, a few people rushed into the office. Two dropped off packages, and one came to pick something up.

Naomi felt like she was in trouble and waiting for her turn to see the principal. She had always known and understood the senator's power, but seeing all of these people working specifically for him gave her a different idea of just how powerful he was.

Nearly thirty minutes later she was still waiting. But she didn't mind. She was prepared to wait all day if she had to. Once Matt confirmed the senator was in the office, she was determined to see him at all costs.

More than an hour into the wait, two big burly men came rushing through the door. They didn't exchange greetings with the receptionist or anyone else but weren't stopped from rushing into the senator's office. A few minutes after that, one of the guys walked out and looked at Naomi.

"Ms. Payne, the senator will see you now."

Naomi wasn't expecting to hear that; her heart skipped a beat. She quickly rose from the sofa and followed him into the senator's office.

When their eyes met, Naomi felt her heart sink. What happened to the love that once shone in his for her? She glanced around the office, surprised to see the two men sitting instead of leaving.

Why weren't they alone? How could he meet with her under these conditions? The man who escorted her into the office had already taken a seat, like she had to meet with a crowd just to talk to the senator. She was fuming, but she refused to let them see her crack.

"Senator?"

"Yes, Ms. Payne, what can I do for you today?" He had the nerve to address her in a sharp professional tone, like she meant nothing.

There was one thing she couldn't deny, despite her anger. He looked good. She noticed a few gray hairs at his temple, but they only enhanced his appearance. He was wearing a chocolate pin-striped suite with a mustard-colored shirt and cuff links she remembered well.

"Calvin?" Naomi fought back tears, her lips trembling as she spoke. Was this the way he was gonna play her? She glanced over at the men sitting off to the side. The one who escorted her in didn't even pretend he wasn't paying attention to them.

"I need to talk to you." She couldn't stop her voice from being shaky. Oh how she wished Sheila was with her; she would definitely know how to handle this situation. But she was alone, all alone, and the reality was she'd just have to suck it up.

"Yes, that's why I understand you're here, to talk to me."

Was he mocking her? He sounded so cold, so uncaring. There was no emotion in his voice. Naomi searched his eyes and looked away when she didn't see the love she was accustomed to seeing there.

Naomi glanced over at the men sitting in the corner; then she looked at the senator, but his expression never changed.

"You did want to see me, correct?"

"Uh, yes. I did. Um, I mean, I still do. I uh, wanted to discuss something real personal with you." She glanced toward the one man who was blatantly staring at her. He didn't even look away when she turned to him. "Well, I was just thinking we could talk in private." She looked at Jim again.

"This is private. You've come to my office unannounced; my aides freed me up to meet with you. So please tell me what it is I can do for you." His jaw tightened, and she noticed.

For some odd reason that slight twitch gave her a sense of hope. Could this all be a facade? Maybe Beverly had learned of their secret and he just had to lie low for a little while. She didn't mean to, but at that very moment, she felt compelled to touch her stomach.

She watched the senator as he watched her. She couldn't read his expression no matter how hard she tried.

"Well, I thought we'd be able to—"

Senator Davis rolled his eyes. He sat up straight, then laced his fingers on top of his desk. "So, Ms. Payne, I have other appointments today. Please let's get to your business, the reason for your visit."

Every word he spoke was like a dagger being plunged straight into her heart. He was handling her. The man she loved, the senator, was handling her! She was appalled. Her eyes began to pool with tears and she fought to hold them back. She'd be damned if he'd get the satisfaction of seeing her cry.

"Well, then." The senator reached into a drawer she couldn't see. Then he stood. "I think this should take care of your problem."

Noami couldn't hide the shock; it was more out of reflex than anything else as she extended her hand and accepted the envelope he passed to her.

"Wh—" Before Naomi knew what was happening the man who had walked her into the office was up and at her side. Before she could say anything he was now all but shoving her out of a side door she didn't notice.

"But I—"

Once outside, Naomi allowed the tears to fall freely. She couldn't remember a time when she'd been so humiliated. She was warm with embarrassment. The senator treated her like common trash. She still didn't want to believe that she had fallen so far off his radar. But the way she was treated confirmed whatever they had was definitely a thing of the past.

It wasn't until she got to her car, nearly forty-five minutes after being tossed out on the street, that she pulled the crumbled envelop from her pocket. She ripped it open only to have her mouth fall to the ground again.

"Twenty-five thousand dollars!" she cried.

She couldn't wait to call Sheila. That bastard! She tucked it back into her pocket when she speed-dialed Sheila's number on her phone.

Sheila answered on the first ring.

"Oh my God!"

"What's wrong with the baby?" Sheila screamed into the phone.

"The baby?" Naomi was momentarily confused.

"Yes, you had a doctor's appointment. The baby, is there something wrong with the baby? Oh God! Don't tell me you did it. You had an abortion! How could you, Naomi?"

"What the hell are you talking about? I am not, I did not have an abortion! I'm in Austin," Naomi admitted bleakly. Again she regretted having made the trip alone.

"What are you doing in Austin?" Sheila screamed. "Austin, how'd you get to Austin?"

"I drove. I drove to Austin this morning to meet with the senator!"

Silence.

"Why didn't you tell me? I would've gone with you."

"I had to do it alone. I had to, and I'm glad I did. I've never been so damn embarrassed in my life!"

"Girl, what did he do?"

"It was what he didn't do."

"Huh? Come again?"

"Sheila, he handled me. Treated me like I was one of his fucking voters, like I was coming in to talk about his campaign or something like that. The whole time, he had both of his fucking bodyguards sitting there, the whole fucking time! In the room with us, while we met!"

"What?" Sheila screamed into the phone.

"Then he had me tossed out on the fucking street! Just like that! Tossed out!" Naomi felt herself getting hot all over again.

"Just like that, huh?"

"I have a right mind to tear up the fucking check he gave me. That oughta show his ass."

"Whoa. He wrote you a check?"

"Yeah, but—"

"But my ass. How much is it for?"

"Um, twenty-five thousand."

Sheila's scream was so loud, Naomi had to move the phone away from her ear.

23

"You did good, boss, don't worry about it. Derrick and me, we're gonna take care of this."

The senator heard what Big Jim was saying. He had no doubt that his guys would rather take bullets than allow any harm to come to him. And it gave him such a sense of relief. He realized he had messed up, but he was also confident his guys would fix this mess. "I just feel bad."

"No need to."

The senator wanted to run to the door and tell her to come back. He wanted to talk, but what to say? Of course the baby was his, but what about Beverly? There was no way in the world she would understand. She'd have her high-powered attorneys sifting through everything he had. The scrutiny from her family alone would be enough to send his career into an early grave.

"You think she's after money?"

Senator Davis leaned back in his massive leather chair. Big Jim sat waiting for the answer.

"You know, I don't think it's about money with her. I really don't."

"Maybe not with her, but that other one, she ain't to be trusted, boss."

"I know, I just wish I knew what the connection was. It just doesn't make sense."

"We're working on her, we'll find out what's going on. Then when we do, Derrick and me, we're gonna take care of it. You shouldn't worry about this."

Senator Davis wasn't really worried about Naomi's friend's agenda. He just wanted the pain in his heart to stop. He had had affairs before, a few one-night stands here and there, a couple of call girls, but there was just something about Naomi. She didn't want anything from him, nothing except some of his time. He knew about women who purposely went after lawmakers; they had a twisted need for power, and saw the pillow talk and other intimate conversations as their way into an exclusive club.

That was not the case with Naomi. He thought back to the first time he even saw her.

It was a hectic day at the school. The senator was there using it as a backdrop for some legislation he was introducing. Moments before the cameras were set to roll, the senator was surrounded by a small group fussing over something on his chest.

"This should get it out," someone said.

"Nah, that's not doing it. What should we do?" another voice asked.

The senator looked up to see a woman walking by. His eyes met hers. Her doe-shaped eyes grabbed and held him tight. Then she smiled and he felt something trigger inside.

"No one has anything to get this stain out?"

one of the people surrounding the senator yelled in frustration.

Naomi walked over to the group. "What's wrong, if you don't mind me asking?"

"Maybe you can help." Senator Davis couldn't stop looking at her pouty lips. He recognized her sex appeal even though she was working hard to cover it up. From what he could see, she had a killer body beneath her conservative outfit. When she smiled, he wanted to tell everyone else to leave immediately.

"What do you have there?" Naomi inquired.

"Grape juice," one of the senator's attendees answered.

"Oh, is that all?" she snickered.

Everyone stopped what they were doing and looked at her.

"You can get rid of this?" Another attendee questioned.

"Lemme just run to my classroom, I'll be back in a flash."

Naomi rushed up to her office and returned as promised with a Tide erase pen.

"You're back!" The senator didn't mean to sound like that. But he had watched the woman, who seemed genuinely friendly.

"I said I had just the thing to help." Naomi held up the pen.

"What's that?"

Naomi took her place in front of the senator and whipped out her pen. She noticed the spot and immediately got to work.

Senator Davis felt something when she was close to him. He filled his lungs with as much of her scent as it could hold. He could smell her shampoo; he sensed a tingle inside, having her so close. He wanted to ask her questions about herself in hopes of getting to know her better, but there were too many people around.

"Okay, see there, it's already going away," Naomi said as she rubbed vigorously at the colored spot on the senator's crisp white shirt.

He couldn't look down at her work, but he trusted she was getting the job done.

A few minutes later she stepped back a bit to inspect her work. She tapped the spot a few times and the senator stole glances into her hypnotizing eyes.

After she cleared up the stain, he went on with the photo shoot. When it was over, he took a call from his wife, who asked how things went. His mind couldn't stay on the conversation as his eyes wandered around, looking for her, but she was gone.

Before they left the campus, he turned to Big Jim and said, "The lady who cleaned up the stain. Make sure she gets the number to my personal cell."

When she called he could've sworn his heart skipped a beat.

24

"Okay, so we're in this together, right?" Sheila tossed Naomi a cockeyed look, then frowned. She already knew she was about to try and get out of it. But Sheila had her eyes on the prize. If the senator would drop twenty-five g's just like that, she knew there was way more where that came from, and she had made it her duty to ensure that they got as much as he was willing or even unwilling to give.

"I'm just a bit confused." Naomi looked more scared than confused. She wasn't sure if that was really the best plan. She heard what Sheila was saying, but still the thought of hurting the senator was a hard pill to swallow. She just couldn't bring herself to agree to do it.

"I don't understand why we have to get the media involved."

Sheila shook her head. She knew the little bitch was scared, but she had worked too hard to have Naomi mess up her plan. And what a plan it was, or was going to be. Now all she needed was for Naomi to do her part and stop acting all scared.

Sheila took a deep breath, sat next to Naomi, and sighed. She didn't want to have to remind the girl that she had driven all the way to Austin and the man wouldn't even give her ten minutes alone with him.

"Look, it's real simple. We've got a week to work this thing out. I'm telling you, you stick with my plan and when it's all said and done, the senator will be begging you to take him back."

Naomi was very uncomfortable with Sheila's thought process; she just didn't see how this plan would do anything but piss the senator off, and that she did not want to do.

"So, you contacted all of the stations?"

"Every last one of 'em, including radio stations and newspapers, and they're hungry for this story. I'm telling you we are on top. Didn't I tell you you were holding the trump card here? So if he doesn't want to talk to you, he doesn't have to, but pretty soon he'll be begging you to talk to him."

"Lemme get this straight." Naomi sat up on the sofa. "You sent them a letter saying you had proof of a state lawmaker who was about to be hit with a paternity suit and that was enough to get them into a frenzy?"

"Girl, yes! We feed them a little at a time. Then when he gets a wiff of it, we wait for him to make a move. I'm telling you, girl, this is the way to handle him. I know his kind, trust that!"

"Ummmm, I don't know about that," Naomi muttered.

Sheila rolled her eyes and slapped her knee. She sighed hard again. This girl didn't know shit. Sometimes it amazed her how naive Naomi could be. At first she told herself the girl was just slow, thought it was an act, but the more time they spent together, she realized it was far from an act. You would think after that long-ass drive to and from Austin she'd want to see him pay.

"What's the problem?"

"Well, for starters, I'm basically threatening him. I mean, for me to hold this press conference, stand up in front of all these cameras, and say I've been having an affair with a married politician is like . . ." Naomi frowned, then shrugged. "I don't know, it's like calling him out or something."

"No, it's like letting him know you mean business, letting him know you're not about to sit back and be treated any ol' kind of way. I mean, damn, look how this man is treating you!" Sheila paused for effect. "He didn't even have the common decency to tell his hired help to get out so you could talk to him in private."

"Yeah, but—"

"But what?" Sheila sucked her teeth. "I'm not telling you to get up in front of the world and say I've been having an affair with Senator Calvin Davis and now that I'm pregnant he won't even talk to me. The only people who will know who you're talking about will be me, you, and the senator."

"Yeah, but—"

Sheila rolled her eyes in a dramatic way. "What now?" she hissed.

"I just don't understand why we've gotta do it like this. I mean, I am not trying to chase the senator away. Remember, my goal is to be with him, I want us to be a family!"

Sheila stared at her blankly. This girl could not be

for real! Did she think this man was about to leave his wife of twenty-something years, and his two kids, not to mention his career, for her ass?

"Naomi, honey, I'm sorry to be the one to tell you this, but the senator, he already has a family, probably don't want the one he got, so I know he damn sure ain't looking for another one. That money he gave you, that money isn't a down payment on your future together, it's hush money. You know, like hush, go somewhere, get rid of the baby, then go somewhere else and hush!"

Naomi started shaking her head. She couldn't help herself, tears started racing down her cheeks. The senator loved her. She knew for a fact he did, she could feel it in his touch, the way he used to talk to her. He just needed to know she wasn't trying to do anything to hurt him.

"I'm trynta tell you. Once the press starts trying to figure out who this man is, he will start to feel the pressure. Girl, at that point, you'll be able to have any damn thing you want. Seriously, I mean anything. What you want, a Hummer? Ooooooh, girl, what about a new wardrobe?" Sheila was laughing, but soon when she realized Naomi hadn't said a word she stopped and looked at her.

"Really, Naomi, what do you want?"

Naomi swallowed hard and looked up at her friend and said, "I want the senator."

25

When Sheila left Naomi she was truly outdone and overly disgusted.

"Really, Naomi, what do you want?"

"I want the senator."

And she had the nerve to actually be serious! Sheila couldn't believe that poor child actually thought, believed for a second that she was anything more than just a fancy piece of ass to Senator Davis. Sheila had to laugh sometimes at all the craziness.

The only thing that kept her from laughing was the sheer severity of her own problems. If she didn't need Naomi to see the light at the end of the tunnel for her own situation, she'd have washed her hands of the foolishness a while ago.

Sheila couldn't leave Naomi's house fast enough. Her tires peeled as she burned rubber turning the block. She was headed straight to her little spot to hit the casino, and if luck was on her side, she could double, maybe even triple her money in a matter of hours. She felt lucky too.

As she drove, Sheila thought about the gold mine

Naomi was sitting on. In the beginning, when they first met, she was excited about having a close female friend. Back then they always talked about men they were seeing and stuff like that. But Sheila was always careful to keep a certain amount of her business to herself. Now all of a sudden things had gotten out of hand and Naomi was her only way out. Shit, she just wanted to pay off what she owed and start fresh.

Sheila decided after her fun at the casino she'd try to talk to David about some figures. She was tired of guessing what they might be willing to offer for her information. The way she saw it, all they had to do was take her information and Senator Davis was certain to do exactly what they wanted.

Sheila swung her car into the full parking lot. She grabbed her large duffel bag of a purse and glanced around the parking lot in both directions before making sure she had enough cash. Sheila was so excited she could hardly walk straight and steady as she walked toward the front door.

"Sheila, how good to see you," the security guard said.

"Hey Steven, I know it's been a minute, but I'm feeling lucky today."

"Well, I hope you're right." He smiled. "I'm sure this is your day. Your lucky day," he said as he pulled the door open for her.

Sheila looked around the room. She noticed familiar faces at the bingo tables, but that was all a front. She slipped through a door in the back and went down a narrow flight of stairs. She entered the room where the real high rollers hung out. A barmaid passed the moment she made her way over to the blackjack table. "Hey, Sheila, where you been, girl?"

"Oh, here and there," she said.

"A panty ripper?" the waitress asked.

"You know it."

"I'll meet you at your spot, right?"

"Girl, you know me too well," Sheila said as she walked to the back where stakes started at one thousand dollars. When Sheila pulled up at her normal spot, the dealer winked at her.

"Jeffery," she said as he shuffled.

Three hours later, Sheila was up five grand. A small crowd had formed around her and she felt great. Something told her this would be her lucky day and she was right. With a panty ripper in one hand, and her fingers from the free hand flipping through her chips, she felt on top of the world.

"Damn, how you feelin', Sheila?" a voice asked.

"Just got paid, so you know I'm living real large-like," she giggled.

At the rate she was going, Sheila had no doubt she'd be able to double her loot before sunup. She was used to bringing up the sun inside the little makeshift casino, and had no problem doing it again. After all, she was on a mission and she had finally reclaimed her lucky streak.

That streak had eluded her for months. After losing big nearly a year ago, she stumbled out of the bingo hall, depressed, broke, and desperate. As luck would have it, she bumped into David at a nearby IHOP. Sheila later learned that meeting was no coincidence. But she was in far too deep to try and back out now and she knew it.

Sheila had just let ten thousand dollars slip

through her fingers after pulling an all-nighter inside the casino. She escaped with twenty dollars in her pocket, and decided she'd go to IHOP to try and figure out how she could possibly get at least half of her money back.

As she was being led to a table in the back, she passed David, who was on his BlackBerry. She was seated next to him and it didn't take long for him to invite himself to her table. Later when she realized she had been his target all along, she didn't know whether to slap or kiss his ass.

By then she decided if they were gonna use her, she'd use them to get what she wanted too. The plan had always been to try and retire from the district with enough money not to have to worry, but every time she got her hands on some money, she headed straight to the casino.

26

This was the first time in a long while Senator Davis made a business-related trip to Houston. Despite how hard he tried, he couldn't shake the uneasiness he felt over the fact that Naomi was no longer in his life.

Images of things they did together, the laughter, the incredible lovemaking all haunted him daily, like a lingering ghost. A part of him died with the end of their relationship, but he had to be smart. He couldn't allow himself to put everything, his family, his career all in jeopardy. He tried to assure himself there would be others. This much he knew, but whether there'd be others like *her* was yet to be seen. Something deep inside told him there would never be another woman to touch him the way Naomi had.

As he enjoyed a martini aboard the jet he turned to Big Jim. "Where are we meeting this guy? You think it's smart that I go with you guys?"

"We can do it either way. I just thought you'd want to be there when we got the 411. But we could just as easily handle it for you." Jim leaned forward as if he'd come up with an even better idea. "Why don't we do this? We could get one of those rooms, where you can sit and listen in a different room while we talk to these jokers. The more I think about it, maybe we should hold off on bringing you in so soon."

The senator eased back to take Jim's words in. He should let them handle it. That's what he had them for, so he didn't have to get his hands dirty.

"I'll be in the next room." The senator nodded in agreement. "I think that's the best way to handle all of this," he concluded.

"Yeah, that way you'll hear everything. The minute we get rid of 'em, we go over the information and you give us, me and Dee, the word and we handle it, fix this for you." Jim slapped his hands together. "Just that simple."

Just that simple. The senator allowed those words to toss around in his head. He wished it really was that simple. Simple would've been no pregnancy and he and Naomi still together. Simple would've been him telling her exactly what she wanted to hear, then easing her into the idea of an abortion. That's what would've been simple, but he had to take the scenic route. Now he and his guys were in the middle of a mess that had the potential of ruining everything he'd worked hard to achieve.

"Boss, we got this, trust us on this one, okay?" Big Jim waited for a response.

The senator opened his eyes and leaned forward. "I can't afford for this thing to get out of hand. I mean, you know what's at stake here, right?"

Derrick chuckled. "You think we can afford to let this thing get crazy, boss? I mean seriously, if you go down we go down, and I don't know about you,

Jim, but I ain't never lived this nice. So you know I ain't 'bout to let no broads ruin what we got going here." Derrick extended a pound to Big Jim.

"That's real. Hell, if need be, we'd go down before you, boss. Just let us handle this."

"You know I'm gonna take care of you guys, you know that, right?"

Derrick and Big Jim looked at each other, then at the senator.

"Shiiiit. You always do, boss, you always do." Big Jim answered.

The Motel 6 near Hobby Airport in Houston wasn't exactly situated in the best part of town. But it was ideal for the kind of business the senator needed handled.

Derrick went to the clerk and paid for the room. He went back to the town car and told the senator which room they were going to be in. The senator walked in and looked around the dark room. He didn't want to be there any longer than the time necessary to figure out what was really going on.

"Good for you?" Big Jim asked.

"Yeah, let's do this shit."

Twenty minutes after Big Jim made the call, the senator took a seat inside the bathroom.

"You hear us?" Derrick asked.

"Yeah, it's good, let's get this shit over with."

About ten minutes into the meeting the senator's ears perked up.

"So she's linked to Armstrong?" he heard Big Jim ask, and he was certain Jim repeated the question for his benefit.

"Indirectly. She's up to her ears in debt, and she owes big. All of a sudden she hooks up with one of their flunkies. We think they targeted her, but either way, she contacts his people, says she's got information for sale. He paid off her first tab. Two months later she's in deeper than before. This time when they go to collect the information she promised, she couldn't produce it. But she's been given an extra sixty days. Since she knows people in high places, my boss wants to give her some time to make good on her promise. Word is she may be able to help Armstrong get back to the capitol. My boss sees the potential in that."

Big Jim knew he had heard enough. He was ready to let the little snitch go. But Derrick wanted more.

"So what happens if she doesn't come through?"

"Oh, that's not even an option. She says she's got something so big, she's all but guaranteeing the race for 2010."

Senator Davis felt like such a fool. How could he have not even considered this mess had something to do with the very career he was trying his best to guard? "So this all leads back to Armstrong?"

"Looks that way, boss, looks that way," Big Jim said.

As they rode to the Hyatt, Senator Davis's head was spinning. All he had to do was get rid of Sheila in the very beginning and he could've avoided this entire mess. Naomi's pregnancy didn't help matters much either, but he could've handled her.

Now that they knew what Sheila was up to, he had to figure out a way to deal with her, especially since he now understood his career depended on it.

27

"Hey, Ms. Lady, I hope you feeling lucky. They been paying out some serious cheddar up in here," the security guard said.

"Whhaaaat?" Sheila smiled.

The bingo hall off Beechnut in southwest Houston was the place to be if you just had to play. The parking lot in front of the hall stayed full twenty-four-seven. To the naked eye that's the only game in town. But for the real high rollers, there was more. A handful of gamblers were invited to the bomb shelter. Back in the day it was built as a refuge for the unpredictable weather that often hit the Gulf Coast. Sheila was no stranger to the bomb shelter.

The guard shook his head. "I was wondering where you been, I ain't seen you in a minute. I was, like, dang, she straight missing out," he added.

"Well, I'm here now," she sang. Sheila wanted to run up into the door. She didn't feel like having small talk, but she didn't want to just blow this dude off. He was always nice to her.

When their conversation trailed off, Sheila

couldn't make it through the doors fast enough. She was speed-walking and nearly ran over her favorite waitress. She didn't have time for more small talk, so she kept moving and claimed her spot at the blackjack table.

Two hours after she arrived, Sheila was on a fierce roll. She was up fifteen thousand dollars and feeling fine. When the waitress came to drop off her fourth pink panty drink, Sheila gave her a hundred-dollar tip.

"Thanks, Sheila. That's whassup," the waitress said as she kissed the chip and put it in her pocket.

"Just working my jelly, Missy, gotta share the wealth," Sheila laughed before she told the dealer to hit her again.

Twenty-four hours after Sheila arrived at the bomb shelter, she was still sitting tight in her chair at the blackjack table and winning. Yeah, she had missed her flight to Vegas, but any true gambler knows you don't leave when the going is good, and Sheila's ass was planted for as long as she was winning. *It's all gravy*, she told herself. Besides, for now she was winning big and she wasn't about to risk changing her luck. Shit, she'd stay a week if her luck allowed it.

The only time Sheila got up was to use the bathroom, and she often held it as long as she possibly could. One time she nearly pissed on herself right there, 'cause she didn't want to get up from her spot.

When she returned to the table, a light-skinned man with a platinum grill and jewelry to match smiled up at her.

"Umm-hmm, lady luck just showed back up," he said toward Sheila.

She wasn't trying to hear what he was saying, though; she was on a roll, and she didn't need some busta trying to hang with a winner. Sheila knew the routine; everybody wants to be your friend when you're winning big. Hell naw, she wasn't looking for any parasites. She didn't even return his bright-ass smile.

Sixteen hours later, Sheila wondered what the fuck had gone wrong. Ever since that wannabe rapper sat next to her, her pile of chips started dwindling. The shit was disappearing fast and his stack was steady growing.

"Hmm, guess you came and lucked up for real, huh?" She sneered in his direction. This time she had to look around his new female friends who had appeared out of nowhere.

"Oh, so now you can holla at a brotha, huh?" He snickered.

Sheila nodded and looked at him, then at her stack of chips sitting neatly in front of him.

"Just say the word and we can blow this joint," he said.

Sheila sucked her teeth. She'd get her win on again. She knew it, and she didn't need to go fuck no broke-down rapper just 'cause he was on top momentarily. Shit, she'd get hers back.

Two hours after that and four thousand dollars lighter, Sheila was hot. Dude was still winning and she was losing fast. She didn't know what to do or what to say. Feeling desperate and frustrated, she leaned over slightly, showing her cleavage.

"I see what you working with. Say, shorty, why don't you let me set you up this time?" he offered.

Sheila couldn't refuse. When she looked down at

the empty space in front of her, all she could do was smile at his offer. She was mad-excited, but wanted to play it cool.

"I 'preciate it, but I'm good for it," she said.

Twelve hours after the initial loan, Sheila had won five thousand dollars. Unfortunately, she owed her new friend twenty thousand dollars. Once again the space in front of her, where stacks of chips once stood, was empty. Sheila felt dejected, she was vexed, but again wanted to try and maintain her composure.

When she looked over at her new friend, he stood. "Damn, girl, you did some real damage up in here. I ain't 'bout to sit here and lose all my money. 'Sides, I'm ready for you to pay up," he said.

Sheila frowned. "What?" she screamed, then looked around.

"Yeah, baby doll, I ain't no bank and trust. Shit, I needs my snaps." Two men appeared at his side and collected his chips. "Y'all cash those in and we'll meet you outside," he said.

"We?" Sheila questioned as she threw him a cutting glare.

"Yeah, baby, you owe a fool twenty grand. That ain't no chump change. So we 'bout to go get my money," he said.

Sheila was panic-stricken, her eyes wide in alarm. "Where the fuck am I supposed to get twenty thousand dollars from?" she asked.

"Now, I'd say that's your problem, but I'm sure if you think about it, you probably got at least one friend who can spot you the money," he offered.

"Huh? Like hell I do. Naw, ain't nobody told your ass to be sitting up in here acting like Big Baller

Bob. Shit, you go' have to wait. I'ma get you your money, but it's gonna take me a minute."

The man looked up at the camera in the ceiling and smiled at Sheila. "Here, why don't we move away from the table? We're done here, I need to holla at you for a minute," he said. He took her by the arm and started walking her toward the door.

Sheila didn't want to go anywhere with him. She started cursing at herself. Why did she even come in here? Shit, the only person she knew with that kind of money was Naomi. How the hell was she gonna get away from them long enough to convince Naomi that she had to cash the check the senator wrote? As she walked out of the bingo hall with her new friend right at her side, the guard looked up.

"Oh, dawg, I see you found her. I told you this her spot, huh, Sheila?"

By the time Naomi pulled up at her apartment she was nice and tired. She looked around because Sheila had said she'd meet her after school. Now, with her being visibly pregnant, it didn't take much to wear her out.

It had been nearly three weeks since she last saw the senator. Naomi was all but ready to give up. She'd have her baby and raise it on her own. If the senator didn't want to be a part of her life or have anything to do with her or their baby, fine.

Sheila had all these ideas about how to bring him down, but when it came right down to it, Naomi knew deep inside, she couldn't do anything to hurt the senator. The one piece of advice she took from Sheila was to cash that check instead of tearing it up.

She did just that. She put all of the money in an account for her unborn child. Life wasn't good without the senator, but she was making it.

Once she settled into the apartment, she walked into the kitchen trying to figure out what to have for dinner. That's when the phone rang.

"Oh my God, Naomi! I'm glad you're there."

"Sheila, is that you? What's going on?"

"Naomi, I, uh, I need a favor. I'm on my way over."

"What is it?"

"I'll tell you when I get there, please don't go anywhere!"

Naomi looked at the phone. The line was dead. "Now what?" She placed the phone back into its cradle. With Sheila it was always something. Naomi couldn't wait to hear what crazy idea or problem she had this time.

28

Senator Davis had heard of prominent people becoming targets simply because of who they were. But never did he think he'd find himself in such a predicament. He admitted, he could've handled Naomi better than he had, but what was done was done; now it was time to take drastic steps to protect and secure his career and family. There was no telling what Armstrong had planned.

Both Derrick and Big Jim had already put the wheels of their plan into motion. Senator Davis agreed, reluctantly, with them that there was no other way. The only stickler was what to do about Naomi. It was obvious she was not going to be deterred from having this baby.

As he entered the capitol he paused for a moment to take in his surroundings. Everything moved at the speed of light. People were rushing in and out of the rotunda; a small protest was taking place on the sidewalk near the capitol's main entrance; then there was the constant sound of traffic, buses hurling by, frustrated drivers leaning on their horns. Senator Davis took a deep breath.

"This is in my blood. I can't allow anything to jeopardize all I've worked for."

"Sir?" Matt turned to look at the senator. "Did you say something?"

The senator tossed Matt a look that said even if he had, it wasn't for Matt's ears. Matt understood the message and knew when it was time to let it go.

He held the door for the senator to walk through, then followed behind him.

By the time the senator arrived at his office, his BlackBerry was vibrating out of control. "Jim, what's the problem?"

"No problem, boss, just wanted to let you know what's going on. It's gonna go down tonight for certain."

"Do you need any additional information?"

"We've got it handled."

"Okay. Oh, by the way, there's no need to call and confirm. You can do the honors in person."

"Cool, boss, but I can assure you it's gonna be handled tonight. So you can think about other things and let us do what you pay us to do."

Finally the senator could see a light at the end of the tunnel. From the moment questions about a baby popped up, he had been uncomfortable. He eased back in his massive leather chair and took a deep breath.

Finally he could begin to get his life back on track. He knew it would be a challenge without Naomi, but he knew and understood in time he'd get over her too.

29

"So you see, I really need that money. I don't know who else to turn to," Sheila sobbed. On her way over, she'd been thinking of the best heart-wrenching story she could come up with to separate Naomi from the money she needed. This one, she determined, would be the best bet.

Naomi was blinking as she tried to understand how Sheila's entire family had no other way of coming up with the money they so desperately needed. She didn't understand how they, Sheila and her two siblings, weren't prepared for an operation they had to have known their ailing mother would need. But she didn't want to seem insensitive either. She kept thinking what things would be like if she were in Sheila's shoes.

"I'm so sorry to even have to ask you for the money. I mean," Sheila sobbed, using the back of her hand to wipe tears from her eyes, "I know it's there for you and the baby, but I promise I'll make sure you get it back, every last dime."

"So how much do you need?" Naomi was so

uncomfortable with this conversation. She didn't know what to say or do, but she figured she needed to get it over with. She knew she'd never see that money again. When Sheila first called to ask for a favor, Naomi thought the favor would be, let's go out together or something like that. Never did she think her friend would be asking for money. She always believed if you loaned someone money, you should just look at it as a donation. She'd spent so much time waiting on borrowed money to find its way back to her. To this day she was still waiting on a few others to pay up.

"Twenty thousand."

Naomi swallowed hard. "Wow!"

"I know it's a lot, I know it is." Sheila was all but shaking while she spoke. "But, Naomi, think about this." Sheila was actually shaking now. "You wouldn't even have that money if it wasn't for me. Remember, you wanted to tear the damn check up. It was me, I'm the one who told you not to do that, I was the one who made you open a savings account for you and the baby, me!"

"Twenty thousand dollars is a whole heck of a lot of money," Naomi said, shaking her head slowly. She was a bit disgusted. She would never, ever ask another human being to *borrow* twenty thousand dollars!

"I know, I understand, but if I had anyone else to go to, I would. I really need your help here." Sheila stopped talking. For a few minutes neither one said a word.

Suddenly Sheila looked up at Naomi. "Haven't I always been there for you? Who did you talk to about the senator? When you didn't know what to do, who did you turn to? I'm just asking, no, I'm begging you to be there for me just this once, the way I've been there for you so many other times before."

"Does your mother not have insurance? I mean, what kind of surgery is this that insurance won't cover?"

"Naomi, I told you already," Sheila hissed. She leaned back in her seat and covered her eyes with her hands. Her shoulders started convulsing as she cried.

Naomi felt awful. She got up and rushed to the bathroom to grab a box of tissue. Was she a monster for not wanting to help her friend? Sheila had done so much to help her. Now this was her chance to repay the favor. When she returned to the living room, she sat next to Sheila. She gave her the tissue and touched her on the shoulder.

"Please stop crying," Naomi begged. She sighed. Sheila looked up at her.

"Do you think I want to be here crying begging you, my friend, for this money? You think I like the idea of my mother needing a surgery and I can't help her out?" Sheila broke down again.

"I know, um, I know this must be hard for you," Naomi said, but she had to struggle to add a bit of sincerity to her voice.

"That money is just sitting there, you don't even need it."

Naomi flinched a bit.

"I mean, I'm sitting here begging, pleading with you for some money that's just sitting in the bank collecting dust. I really thought we were better than this."

"We are—"

Sheila jerked away from Naomi, stopping her midsentence. She shot daggers at her and with quivering lips said, "Obviously we're not!" Sheila wiped her eyes again and got up from the sofa. She headed for the door.

"Wait, Sheila."

Naomi's voice stopped Sheila cold in her tracks. She stood there for a moment, with her back to Naomi. This was far more difficult than she had expected. She hadn't expected her to just fork over the cash, but she also hadn't thought she'd have to beg. "What?"

"I'll lend you the money. But you have to pay me back," Naomi said firmly.

For a second Sheila didn't say a word. She didn't even respond. She turned to Naomi and smiled. "Are you serious? You mean it?"

Naomi nodded. "It's like you said. I was gonna tear up the damn check anyway. You're the one who told me not to and convinced me to open that account. Besides, it's just money. I don't want money to come between us."

Sheila stepped toward Naomi. "I'm so lucky to have you as a friend. I thank you, but more importantly, my mother thanks you."

"Okay, well, you know I can't get the money until tomorrow."

Sheila frowned. "Why not till tomorrow?"

"Um, because we're talking twenty thousand dollars here. Besides, the bank's probably closed by now, and I'm waiting—"

"The bank inside Kroger isn't closed. They stay open till six or seven!" Sheila persisted. She didn't

want to seem too anxious, but she needed to get her
hands on that money as quickly as possible; a life
really did depend on it.

Naomi frowned. "Wait a minute. It's not like your
mother could use that money right this minute. I
mean, I've already said I'm gonna lend you the
money, but I can't get to it until tomorrow. Why isn't
that good enough for you? Besides, like I was saying,
I'm waiting for the guy to come and fix my Internet.
It's down."

"Oh." Sheila retreated. She really didn't want to
wait for the money, but the more she thought about
it, waiting a few hours wasn't that big of a deal. The
real issue was that she could finally pay off her debt;
then she could get back on track and move along
with her plans.

"Well, I know how those cable people can be.
What did they give you, a window of twelve to
two?"

"Two to six, girl." Naomi chuckled.

"I can't stand 'em." Sheila gave Naomi a hug.
She looked at her once they broke the embrace and
said, "I'm sorry about all that stuff earlier. I really
do appreciate your help."

"Don't worry about it. That's what friends are
for, right?"

"Thank you, girl."

Sheila picked up her bag and prepared to leave.
She was seconds from grabbing the doorknob when
Naomi said, "Oh, what's the name of the hospital?
I'll need it because that's who they'll write out the
cashier's check to."

"Cashier's check," Sheila asked awkwardly.

Shit, she hadn't thought about that. She thought Naomi understood she needed cash!

"Yeah, you don't think I'd go take twenty thousand dollars in cash out of the bank, did you?"

Sheila's face dropped.

30

"She cannot be that stupid!" Senator Davis had just finished watching the exchange between Sheila and Naomi. A part of him didn't really care what she did with the money, but the fact that she'd fall for something that ridiculous made him feel like a bit of a fool himself.

"Her mother needs an operation; she couldn't come up with anything better than that?" He shook his head at the stupidity.

Big Jim will take care of this mess, Senator Davis thought with great satisfaction. The two had never let him down. The senator thought about the dedication he had from Jim and Derrick. They'd helped him with several discreet situations in the past. The most recent was helping out a fellow senator.

It was right after summer break last year. Senator Goodman's teenaged son found himself in a bit of trouble after a senior trip. The senator thought about how things could've gone so wrong.

"It's my boy," Senator Goodman's frantic voice had said through the phone. The call pulled Senator

Davis from his sleep. It took him a while to catch his bearings.

"Who's this? Thomas? That you?"

"Yeah, Calvin. I'm sorry to call at this ungodly hour, but my boy. They went on a senior trip. You know he's been accepted at Stanford, we can't let this happen, it'll ruin him! Every damn thing he's worked so hard for!"

"Calm down, what are you talking about? What's going on? What's gonna ruin him?"

"A girl, some tramp, is crying rape, says my boy and three of his friends raped her. You know Devon, he's a good boy. You know he don't have to do nothing like that. I can't tell you how many phone calls we get from these girls always calling this boy, basically throwing pussy at him. My boy don't have to do anything like what they're saying."

"Okay, look, calm down, where's Devon right now?"

"They got him down at county."

"What?"

"He just called me. We don't know what to do. We're gonna call the lawyer, but I just wanted to see if there's anything you can do to help. We don't want the press to get a hold of this thing. You know what'll happen then."

Senator Davis turned on his night-light and pulled himself up from bed. "I'm gonna call you back in thirty minutes. Don't call your lawyer just yet. Give me thirty."

Beverly stirred, but she didn't wake.

"Okay, but you know my boy ain't used to nothing like this."

"Thirty minutes!"

Senator Davis left the room and went to his study. He picked up his BlackBerry and called Big Jim.

"Whassup, boss?"

"I've got a situation here."

"You need me to come over?"

"No, let me tell you what's happened."

The senator told Jim the story just the way Senator Goodman had relayed it to him. He didn't know what Jim would do, but he knew Jim would fix it. He and Derrick could solve any problem, it didn't matter the nature. And the best part was, once the senator turned things over, he never had to worry about them again.

By the time Big Jim was done, both the girl and her gold-digging mama had fully recanted their story. They were able to keep the whole mess under the radar and away from the press. The last Senator Davis had checked with Senator Goodman, Devon was thriving at Stanford and expecting to graduate early and then enter law school.

The phone rang, pulling the senator's thoughts back to work and his own mess. He made it his business to remain in Austin, and remain visible because he didn't want to be tied to anything that might happen. Big Jim, Derrick, and the senator all agreed, the less he knew, the better for everyone involved.

"Senator Davis, your lunch appointment is here." It was Matt. The senator wondered if the caterers had already arrived with the food. Senator Davis had accepted an invitation by Mothers for Religion in Schools' president and secretary. When the ladies tried to meet him at a restaurant, he explained he had a full schedule and wouldn't be able to leave the capitol. He immediately sensed the disappointment on their faces, and said, "But that doesn't mean I can't have food brought here into the office."

Anyone watching the senator over the last few days would've seen a dedicated and busy man at work. He met with a local middle school class Monday morning. The following day, he hosted a Boy Scout troop at the capitol, and in addition to his meeting with the Bible Mothers he was scheduled to attend a ground breaking ceremony later that afternoon for a new transitional housing project for battered women.

Despite a tight and busy schedule, his mind still lingered on the outcome of his peculiar situation with Naomi. He told Jim and Derrick to handle it however they saw fit, but that didn't stop him from wondering who would still be standing once the dust finally cleared.

31

Sheila's small apartment still showed signs of the break-in that had happened weeks ago. As she got out of her car, she thought about being able to repay her debt and moving on with her life.

She'd planned to get paid, quit her job, and move far away from Houston. But she also knew Naomi and her cooperation were key to the success of her overall plan.

As she unlocked and opened her front door, she pulled out her cell phone and dialed a number. The phone rang two times before a man's voice answered.

"Hey, what's going on?"

"You tell me."

"Look, David, I know there's been a bit of a set-back, but I'm getting back on track. I just want to make sure we're still on the same page here. I need to make sure I'll be properly compensated for my hard work, not to mention the ultimate betrayal of a friend."

"Yeah, some things are priceless," David snarled.

"Anyway, you tell the senator my price has just gone up. I need to protect my interests, not just today, but for the future, period."

"So what are you talking about here?"

"Look, I'm about to deliver in a huge way. I just want to make sure I get what's coming to me. I don't want to have any problems once you guys get what you want, and not to mention, I need to make sure I'll be set up nicely."

"You're still not telling me what you want."

Sheila pushed the door with her hip as she reached for the light switch and flicked it, but nothing happened. There was a little light flooding in from the hall, but not enough to help her see clearly.

"Damn, the lights are out."

"What did you say?"

"Wait, hold on a moment," she said to David.

Sheila walked farther into the apartment. Then suddenly there was a blow to the back of her head.

"Oooouch! What the fuck!"

It wasn't hard enough to do too much damage, but her legs wobbled a bit and she dropped the cell phone.

"Sheila?" David's voice screamed through the cell phone, but he didn't hang up.

The second blow came and knocked her clean off her feet.

"You like to gamble, huh, bitch! You should learn to pay your debts!"

Wham! Wham!

"No! Please! I'll have the money! I swear, I'll have the money!" she shrieked. The back and side of her head were pounding. Although the room was still dark, bright stars danced in front of her eyes. Sheila threw up her arms, hoping to block the blows.

"Too late! You've had enough time." The final blow sent her into an abyss of complete darkness.

David sat quietly on the other line. He had heard the entire assault, but there was nothing he could do to help.

Blood oozed from the side of Sheila's head as the dark shadow stooped down to pick up her purse. He dug up the digital recorder, then ran to the back of the apartment.

The next day when Sheila didn't show up for work, Naomi figured she must've been at the hospital taking care of her mother. But she remembered Sheila never did mention which hospital her mother was in.

During her lunch break she went to the bank and got a cashier's check made out in Sheila's name. After Sheila had explained the check shouldn't be made out to the hospital because it might need to have the insurance company's name on it, Naomi thought it best to leave it blank. The bank informed her that they couldn't do that, so she opted for Sheila's name.

As she approached the front door, she thought it odd that it was open. Naomi looked down the hall in both directions. Why would Sheila's door be wide open like this? It was the middle of the afternoon, and her front door was wide open; something seemed out of place.

"Sheila?" Naomi called out to her. She pushed the door open with her foot, then looked down and screamed.

"Oh my God! Sheila!" Naomi grabbed her friend by the shoulder and shook her.

When Sheila didn't respond, she rushed inside and dialed 911. It wasn't until she walked back over to Sheila's body that she noticed the pool of blood by the left side of her head.

It didn't take long for police and emergency workers to flood Sheila's apartment. Officers had Naomi out in the hall as they questioned her about what she knew.

"When did you see her last?"

"She left my house last night. I was just coming over here to bring her some money for her mother's surgery," Naomi said.

The officer jotted down everything she said, so quickly at times Naomi began to feel a bit uncomfortable.

Naomi couldn't believe Sheila was dead. She wondered, then pushed the thought from her mind. Could her friend have been killed because of her relationship with the senator? Nah, what were the odds of that? Naomi shook the thoughts from her mind.

32

Senator Davis wasn't ready to get up. He wanted more sleep because in his dream, he was on a sandy white beach, and he was running. He was running fast. He couldn't tell where he was running to, but soon, once the fog cleared, he noticed Naomi was running toward him.

"Baby?"

Was someone calling him? Who could it be, was it Naomi while they were running? It was so early in the morning, he and Naomi were going to watch the sunrise together. But that wasn't Naomi's voice. No, he wanted to go back to the beach, where Naomi was running toward him. Would he be able to catch up to her? How long would they have to run, and why hadn't he caught up to her? Could they recapture their earlier relationship?

"Baby?"

It wasn't Naomi's voice and he wasn't on the beach. The senator opened his eyes. He looked upward and noticed the ceiling; then his eyeballs turned to the left, and when he saw the pastel-colored walls he knew exactly where he was. The whiny voice confirmed it too.

"You said we could go to San Marcos today and shop until I can't anymore."

Beverly. The senator closed his eyes. Oh how he missed Naomi. He missed her so much at times he wanted to throw caution to the wind and call her. Or at least he wanted to call her and say something this time. He had called several times. He blocked his number and when she answered, he'd listen to her say hello a few times and then he'd hang up. He often wondered if she suspected him as the culprit.

When his wife planted kisses all over his face, he could no longer pretend to be asleep or sleepy. Lately Beverly had been behaving strangely. He didn't know what to make of it, but there was that part of him that really didn't even care. Something in him had died when he had to let go of Naomi, and the sight of his wife reminded him of what he had lost. "Can't you call some of your girlfriends?"

"But you said—"

"I know what I said. I've got a meeting today, have the driver take you. I don't have time to go running around while you shop. And what's been with you lately?" Senator Davis didn't wait for his wife's answer. He padded across the massive room's floor and walked into the bathroom. As an afterthought he locked the bathroom door, not wanting her to take advantage of any opportunities.

In the shower, he longed for Naomi. He couldn't remember the last time he had shed a tear, but he'd come very close in the last few weeks. That's when he'd been at his most vulnerable state. He wanted to make things right, but he wasn't sure if it was too late. And the fact that he hadn't received any kind of update from Big Jim made this situation even worse. When he thought about it, they all agreed, there would be no need to speak of anything. It was the only way to keep the senator's image squeaky clean.

Nearly thirty minutes after he had locked the door, Senator Davis emerged a new man. The shower was revitalizing, just what he needed.

As he entered the bedroom, he was looking at his wife's back. Earlier she had been excited about a shopping trip. Now she sat at the bed's edge, shoulders slumped and head hanging low. He was so tempted to walk out as if he didn't even notice her, but knew he couldn't. There was no telling what kind of drama he'd open himself up to if he decided to walk out.

Shit! Now what? The senator dragged himself to the other side of the room.

"Bev? What's going on? I thought you were going shopping."

His wife looked up at him, her eyes pooling with fresh tears.

"Are you having a baby?" she asked.

33

Naomi didn't know what to do or who she could trust. Why was her friend dead? And what about the plan? What if Sheila had confided in someone else? Maybe she should call the senator. No, she quickly dismissed that option, but who else could she trust? She was not about to go through with this press conference now that Sheila was gone! What would she look like? She hadn't even agreed with the plan when Sheila was trying to talk her into it.

Nearly four months pregnant now, Naomi had never felt so alone in her entire life. She placed a hand on her budding stomach and looked down. "What a fine mess!"

Usually, she'd be able to pick up the phone and call Sheila for some off-the-wall advice or just to vent. Now there was no one to call.

As she sat in her living room feeling helpless, she wondered what would happen to her and her baby. The phone rang and she looked in its direction. She wasn't expecting any calls. She'd taken time off from work, so it couldn't be the job. Naomi considered allowing her machine to pick up, then had decided to let it when there was a loud knock at her front door. It was so loud she jumped. She'd been on the edge ever since she went and discovered Sheila's body in her apartment.

"Yes?" she yelled through the closed door. Naomi looked through the peephole and saw a man holding up a badge. Her heart sank. She started feeling nervous, but she wasn't sure why. What the hell? Maybe the police wanted to talk to her about what had happened with Sheila. Quite surely she didn't have any information that could help with their investigation.

"I'm Detective Jones, looking for Ms. Naomi Payne." Detective Jones was a tall man with an average build. His face looked rough with a scar near his right eye. Could she pretend not to be Naomi today?

Naomi stood at the door, with it cracked slightly open. "Um, can I see that badge again?"

He pulled it out, and flipped it over so she could see his ID as well. Naomi moved to the side and allowed him in.

"Please come in, but I'm not sure what I can do for you."

Detective Jones looked around her apartment at the sofa, table, and TV set. She lived modestly. He'd already been by her job and she wasn't living beyond her means from what he could see.

"Would you like to have a seat?"

"Nah." He shook his head. "Ms. Payne, I have a few questions about your friend Sheila's death." There was no point in beating around the bush.

Naomi grimaced. She didn't care if he felt like standing, she needed a seat. She turned and sat on the wing chair near the coffee table. She struggled not to look guilty, even though she hadn't done a thing. She also found it hard to remain calm. She took a deep breath and convinced herself she could answer his questions, whatever they were.

"How well did you know Ms. Carson?"

Although she knew she hadn't done a thing wrong, Naomi couldn't help but feel like she was in some sort of trouble.

"Um, well, we work together. Um, I mean, we met at work, worked together for something like five years, I think." Naomi shrugged. She was fidgeting and couldn't stop.

"I didn't ask how *long* you've known her, I asked how *well* you knew her."

Naomi started blinking. She didn't understand what he was trying to say. This was no time for trick questions. If she knew Sheila for five years, didn't that mean she knew her well enough? "I suppose you can say we knew each other, um, kinda pretty well."

Detective Jones's right eyebrow inched upward, his head tilted ever so slightly. "Either you knew her well or you didn't Which is it?"

"Uh," Naomi muttered. "I knew her well," she finally said.

"Did you know about her gambling problem?"

"Eh, gambling problem?" Noami shook her head slowly. "We used to go play bingo every once in a while, when we were bored. But I'd hardly call that a gambling problem."

"Ms. Carson was fifty thousand dollars in the hole with the Conflenti brothers. Do you know anything about them?"

Naomi shook her head. *Sheila gambling? Owing mobsters?* This had to be some kind of mistake.

"Well, she was able to pay off thirty grand quite suddenly actually, but she still owed twenty—"

"Her mother's operation!" Naomi screamed.

Detective Jones shot her an awkward glance, and jotted something else down in his notepad. "Ma'am?"

"Sheila, um, she came to me the night before she died—"

"Was killed," Detective Jones corrected. "She was murdered, Ms. Payne, your friend was murdered."

"Well, um, yes, that's right. Well, the night before that, she came to me and told me she needed money for an operation for her mother. I didn't understand because she never spoke about her mother before, so anyway, she came to borrow twenty thousand dollars from me."

Detective Jones looked around her apartment again. He listened to her story.

"And you had twenty thousand dollars to loan her?"

An eyebrow went up slightly, but Naomi noticed it. "Um, yes," she said slowly and softly.

She noticed his eyebrow clearly going up, and swallowed hard. How would she say she had the money because her married former boyfriend, the senator, wrote her a check to get rid of her and his illegitimate baby?

"Look, Ms. Payne, your friend was involved in quite a few shady dealings. Now we're trying to figure out how much of a role you may have played in her blackmailing scheme."

Horror was etched into Naomi's features.

"Blackmailing scheme?" she repeated.

"Yes, and if you played a major role, or even a minor role, your life could be in danger. Let's not even mention the possible charges. So I need you to be straight with me, because from what we can tell, your friend was messing with some pretty powerful and dangerous people. She was in way over her head, and I can't stress this enough, what happened to her"—his finger was pointed toward her—"you could be next."

Naomi's mouth dropped.

"Your life could be in danger."

Her heart was gripped with fear.

"You could be next."

34

Senator Davis was seething as his shaking hands held the letter his wife, Beverly, had clutched to her chest. It took some firm words, but he was finally able to pluck it from her hands.

"What the hell is this?" His jaw tightened. His eyes couldn't move along the page fast enough. He thought for sure he'd have a natural fit.

"You believe this shit?" He scowled at his wife.

She shrugged beneath his scrutiny.

He waved the letter in the air. "I can't believe this foolishness."

He turned to leave, but stopped when his wife said, "For years I've looked the other way."

Senator Davis didn't respond. His heart was beating rapidly and he felt a thin layer of sweat blanket his forehead.

"You don't think I know. I probably remember them all. I'm no fool, Calvin. I know I no longer do it for you. But for Christ's sake! A baby? How could you?"

Senator Davis spun around on his heel. He rushed

to his wife's side. He felt love for her, but not the burning desirable kind of love. Not the kind of love that made him want to scoop her into his arms and kiss her until her body begged for more. What he felt for Beverly was a very strong sense of respect.

"We have children! What will people say?"

"Honey—" he began.

"Oh, save it, Calvin!"

"There is no baby! Look at this." He waved the letter again. "Do you see my name here? Do you see anything that says this is me? Where'd you get this from anyway?"

Beverly looked at her husband, but she couldn't believe a word he was saying.

"Think about it. I mean, what does this say?" He turned to the letter and began reading aloud.

"Your husband's been quite busy. Now his girlfriend is pregnant and that means he's about to become a daddy once again. If you don't believe me, just watch the news next Monday, October twenty-ninth. If you miss the news, then just pick up a paper. We're sure this will make front-page news statewide." Senator Davis was exasperated. "C'mon, honey, don't tell me you believe this mess?" he chuckled.

But in the back of his mind, he wanted to put his hand around Naomi's neck and squeeze the life from her body. How could she betray him like this?

Maybe it wasn't her, maybe it was that friend of hers. He had to call Big Jim. But as he looked at his wife, who had once again broken down, he knew he couldn't leave her any time soon.

"I promise you, this is just some sick game. This has nothing to do with me. I'm not sure how you got this, but I'll get to the bottom of it, and I'll make sure you get a public apology!"

She looked at him skeptically.

He knew he had to keep it together long enough to get to Big Jim. He just hoped it wouldn't be long.

When the phone rang, he dreaded the thought. There was no telling who that could be. When it rang again, his wife jumped up and rushed to it.

"Davis residence. I've got it, Madeline," she said to the housekeeper, who had picked up the other line.

"Davis residence," she repeated once she heard the housekeeper hang up.

"Lynn, oh my!" she howled into the phone.

Senator Davis rolled his eyes. If she was about to gossip with another senator's wife, maybe, just maybe, he'd be able to sneak out and call Big Jim. He had to take care of this. He all but promised he would, and Big Jim had never failed him before.

"Now what?" he heard his wife say. She turned to him. "Calvin, Lynn got a similar letter, and she tells me Senator Armstrong's wife did too, and Senator Dixon's wife." Beverly's free hand flew to her hip.

"Didn't I tell you this was nothing more than a crazy prank? I told you, I'll get to the bottom of it!"

"It just doesn't make sense," Beverly said.

Senator Davis wasn't sure if she was talking to him or to Lynn on the phone. But one thing he knew for sure, he had highly underestimated both Sheila and Naomi.

35

Fear forced Naomi to make some changes. When Detective Jones ran through the sordid details of Sheila's scheme, using her and her unborn child as the focal point, she knew it was no longer safe to be in her own home.

The detective told her it would take some elbow grease to get her the kind of protection she needed. But he promised he'd work on it right away. Naomi was no fool, she was not about to stay there like a sitting duck waiting for someone to come in the night and kill her and the baby.

The detective had given her his card, even written his cell number on it, and told her to call anytime. But Naomi had a better plan. The moment he walked out of her apartment, she got up and started packing. She wasn't taking much, but enough. She needed to be someplace safe until they found out exactly who had killed Sheila and why.

The first stop she made was to the bank, where she pulled out twenty thousand dollars in cash and paid for a safe-deposit box. Inside the box she put fifteen thousand in cash and kept the other five.

Once that was done, she went back home, parked her car, and used her cell to call for a rental.

Naomi didn't quite know where she was going, but she knew she needed to get away from her place. She couldn't really leave the city because Detective Jones wanted to keep her abreast of the investigation.

For now, a hotel would do just fine, something far enough away where no one would think to look for her. She drove to the north side and checked into a hotel under a false name, the way she used to do when she and the senator were sneaking around. The room was nowhere near as grand as the suite she used to cozy up with the senator in, but for now, she figured it would have to do.

When Naomi awakened the next morning, she still couldn't believe how she was stuck in the middle of this mess. The first thing she did was pick up the phone and call Detective Jones.

She got his voice mail.

"This is Naomi Payne. Um, I'm just calling to let you know I had to leave home for a few days while my place is being exterminated. So if you need to reach me, please call my cell." She left her cell number, then hung up. She eased back on the bed and decided, she'd have to figure out her next move.

Naomi was bewildered. Each time she thought about everything the detective had told her, she wondered how you could think you know someone so well and not really know a damn thing about them. At first, she refused to believe her good friend and confidante would do the things he was talking about.

But when Detective Jones pulled out his evidence, she was nearly blown away. Who all had gotten those letters? And was Sheila really about to scam money out of all of those people? According to the records Sheila kept, a total of seven senators or their wives had received those letters, or were set to. The letters were only the first phase of the plan. Once they got the letters, Naomi would go on TV to say to the world she was pregnant by a senator. By then the plan was for Sheila to contact each of the senators' wives and offer her a way to save her husband's career. If they agreed to send the money, she would make sure news of the infidelity and subsequent child never surfaced.

"It was quite a plan," Detective Jones had said.

But the saddest part was, Naomi had no clue how she was being used. She thought the press conference was going to scare the senator back into her arms. Or at least that was the way Sheila had explained it.

"Once he knows you're prepared to play hardball, shit, girl, he'll come running back to you," she had said.

It took some time, but finally Naomi was able to convince Detective Jones that she had nothing to do with Sheila's elaborate plan. She told him all about her pregnancy by a married man, but refused to identify him. She simply said the relationship had been over long before she learned she was pregnant and she assured him, she was not pregnant by a senator.

As far as she could tell, he believed her, or at least he seemed as though he believed her, and that was good enough for her. She didn't need him thinking she was planning to blackmail anyone.

Naomi thought about the way things were turning out. She missed the senator so much she didn't know what to do, but she also realized that what they had had was over. He had had so much opportunity to make up for what had gone wrong with them, but he hadn't.

36

"What the hell is she up to?" Senator Davis was breathing flames, his nostrils were flaring, and his eyes were on fire.

"Boss, we will shut her down."

"Look at this!" The senator slammed the crumpled letter on the table. It took some time, but he had managed to calm Beverly down. What he didn't want was for his wife to start talking to his in-laws. Her father, now retired, still yielded quite a bit of power. Now as Senator Davis stood in his office, he had already told Big Jim and Derrick he was not concerned with whatever they had done, but he was desperate to find out what Naomi was going to do next.

"Okay, let me tell you what we've found out so far. She was scheduled to do a news conference. The friend set it up. They were going to announce that Naomi was pregnant with a senator's baby and the senator, who's married, dropped her when he found out."

Senator Davis closed his eyes and sighed. He couldn't bring himself to believe Naomi would purposely set out to hurt him. Because that's exactly what that would do, it would destroy him, his family, and his career.

"She was gonna talk to the press?" the senator asked for clarification.

"The plan was to target the wives. Drop them a warning letter saying hey, if you enjoy your comfortable life as a senator's wife, you might want to hear us out."

"Who all got the letter?"

"Seven of you, but this is a good thing," Big Jim quickly added.

"How so?" The senator was confused, his frustration mounting by the second. He couldn't see anything good about him and his peers being blackmailed by his former mistress.

"Because, out of seven, at least three or four of the targeted men are having or have had a dip on the side. You know what that means, right?"

Senator Davis failed to see the reason for the smile that stretched across Big Jim's face. So he simply shrugged; he was near the end of his rope.

"That means there are at least three, if not more, men who may want to see Sheila and Naomi dead."

Those words should've brought him a sense of satisfaction or even relief, but they didn't. Instead he thought about what Derrick and Big Jim were saying. Did they really have to do something to Naomi? Did she have to be hurt in order to save him? Maybe he was just overreacting. As usual, he'd allow the guys to handle their business. "I never looked at it like that."

"That's why we're on the job, boss. You don't have to think about it like that. We don't even want

you to. You just sit back and allow us to handle this."
Big Jim looked at the senator for a few lingering
minutes. "You cool with that?"

The senator didn't respond right away. There was
so much he wanted to say or ask. A part of him didn't
want Naomi to get hurt. He wanted to make sure she
didn't see the same fate as Sheila, but he knew he
couldn't say anything remotely close to that. Suddenly something rendered them all speechless. They
focused on the TV, which had been playing in the
background, virtually unnoticed until now.

"This is a Channel 42 newsbreak so that we may
bring you late breaking news."

Big Jim looked at the senator and he looked at
the screen.

"This is breaking news from the K-eye newsroom. The K-eye newsroom has just learned a state
senator is accused in a paternity lawsuit."

"How'd they get—"

The senator's hand cut Big Jim off midsentence.

They sat and watched as the news anchor went
to a reporter who was standing right outside the
capitol.

"Keith, what have you learned so far?"

"Well, Maggi, the wives of seven senators have
received letters just like this one." The reporter held
the letter close to the camera.

"It basically says, your husband has an illegitimate child on the way. Either you pay up or we'll go
public."

"Shit! The press is already on it!" Senator Davis
buried his head in his hands.

Big Jim looked at the screen. He listened to exactly what the reporter said, then turned to his

boss and said, "With the other one gone, they'll be looking for her now. She's gotta go. We can't run the risk of her talking, not to his camp or to the press in Houston. What do you want us to do?"

Senator Davis raised his head. He looked at the reporter, then back at Big Jim.

"Just give us the word, boss, and we'll take care of this. You know we will. We've already heard from the Missus, whatchu' say?"

"We've gotta get to her before they do," the senator said softly.

Big Jim rose from his seat. "You know what this means, right? We can go after her."

The senator brushed him off with the wave of a hand. "Just take care of it! Fix this!"

He knew exactly what he was saying, and although his heart broke with every word of his command, his brain told him there was simply no other way. Naomi, he decided, had brought all of this on herself! Besides, the few words his wife had spoken were loud and very clear; he'd fucked up and she expected him to make things right.

37

As she moved out of the elevator, Naomi glanced around in confusion. The lobby was overflowing with people. Most of them were wearing name badges and carrying small tote bags. She walked up to the front desk and asked the clerk, "What's going on here?"

"National Real Estate regional meeting." She smiled perkily.

"Oh, I see." Naomi turned and looked around the crowded lobby. This wasn't necessarily a bad thing. With more people crawling around, quite surely it would be more difficult to spot her.

She turned and walked out of the lobby. Her plan was to go to the police department and meet with Detective Jones. She was hoping to get some answers from him, so she could decide what she should do next.

Charlie Watson had lived a hard life. At five feet eight inches tall, with a stocky body, he was able to blend in with many crowds. Most of his forty-eight years were spent doing hard time and he wasn't afraid to go back to prison. Fresh off a nine-year stint, he was eager for work. He was known for doing the kind of work most people wanted done but were never brave enough to do.

The moment Naomi walked toward the parking lot, Charlie moved too. When she first walked out, he pulled his picture to make sure she was the one he was supposed to follow. He grabbed his cell phone and dialed a number. "She just walked out of the hotel."

"Can you take her?"

"Too crowded, some kind of convention or something going on, the place is crawling with people."

"Where is she now?"

"Walking toward the parking lot."

"Parking lot? More than one level?"

"Yeah. Oh, shit, wait. Now she's coming back."

"Can she see you?"

"Nah, way too many people, taxis all over the place. I'm good."

"I don't know what to tell you, but we need to get this taken care of."

"I'm on it. Damn!" the man yelled.

"Whassup?"

"She just climbed into a cab. Shit! I can't get to it." Charlie started running, but it was too late. Six or seven cabs had pulled up by the time he ran toward the pickup point in front of the hotel.

He was breathing hard.

"You need a cab?" the hotel worker asked.

"Shit! No!" he screamed.

"So she's gone?"

"Yup, damn!"

"It's not all lost. Find out which room she's in. And by the end of the day we don't wanna have to worry about her anymore. Obviously she's coming back to the room, so you just sit there and wait."

Charlie walked back to his car and popped his trunk. He looked around before digging into a bag. He pulled out a badge and grabbed a blazer from the backseat. He walked back into the hotel and up to the registration desk.

"I'm Detective Robinson," he lied, smiled, and quickly flashed his badge. Then he pulled out the picture of Naomi. "We're looking for this woman. We know she's staying here, but we need access to her room."

"Oh, of course, Detective." The clerk went to work to retrieve information about Naomi. Once she found the information, she pressed a button on her phone and called her manager.

A few minutes later, the hotel manager came up to the desk.

"This is my manager, Detective." She turned to the manager and said, "This is Detective Robinson, he needs access to one of our guests' room."

"Ah yes, I've got the key, but hotel policy is we must escort you up."

"That's fine," Charlie said.

He followed the hotel manager up to the second floor and stood by while the manager used his card key to enter Naomi's room. The manager walked all the way in. When his phone rang, he looked at Charlie as if he wanted permission to answer. Charlie said, "Oh, I need to use the facilities anyway."

The moment the manager turned his back and

started yelling into the phone, Charlie slipped something into the room door's lock.

Inside the cab, Naomi rubbed her belly. She never thought she would wind up a single parent. No one to share late night feedings with; she'd have to do it all alone. She leaned back in the seat and decided she'd be okay. She damn sure wasn't the first woman to raise a child alone.

When the taxi pulled up in front of the HPD storefront in the Montrose area, Naomi leaned forward to pay her fare, then hopped out.

"You want me to wait?"

"Oh, thanks but no, I'll be fine."

She opened the doors to the police department and walked inside.

"Hi," she said to the officer sitting behind the counter. "I'm here to see Detective Jones."

"Is he expecting you?"

"Um, no, but I was hoping to get some information from him."

The officer turned back to the computer screen.

Just as Naomi was about to break into a long, drawn-out explanation, she turned to the sound of her name.

"Ms. Payne?"

"Detective Jones!"

He looked a bit bewildered, but Naomi smiled as if he should've been pleased to see her.

"I was wondering if you learned anything more about Sheila, you know, what's going on?"

"Here, why don't you come on back so we can talk?"

Naomi walked behind the counter and followed

Detective Jones into a small office. She was torn between telling him everything and waiting to see if he'd gotten any closer to finding out the truth on his own.

"Are your eyes hazel?" Naomi felt like a fool the moment the words fell from her lips. She had been thinking it, and wondering why she didn't notice this before. Detective Jones's head tilted ever so slightly.

"Ah, yeah, they are," he said.

"Sorry." She felt silly.

"Don't worry about it." He smiled.

38

"Take care of it, the moment she walks in."

Charlie replayed the instructions in his mind over and over again. He'd been hiding out inside Naomi's hotel room wondering what the hell was taking her so long. He thought about how smoothly he had handled the manager and wanted to give himself a pat on the back.

"Did you find everything you needed?" the manager had asked.

"Yes, thank you."

Before leaving the hotel Charlie made sure he was seen by the manager and the clerk who originally helped him. He went outside, hopped in a cab, and took a drive a few blocks away. Once he was dropped off, he walked across the street and called for another taxi.

This time when he returned to the hotel, he went directly to his car. He changed his clothes, then walked back into the hotel through a side door. Charlie went to the second floor, and with ease let himself back into Naomi's room. That's where he had been for the past three hours.

Once this one was bagged, he'd make a sweet ten grand, and he was certain this would be just the beginning. Charlie knew men like his boss. They couldn't stay out of trouble even if they tried. He already understood the rules: when you got money, you think you're above the law or should be. But Charlie didn't mind that line of thinking at all; it just meant more work would eventually be flowing his way.

After watching Naomi, he decided he might just have a little fun with her before he handled the business. There was no point in letting a sweet little ass like hers go to waste. No, first he'd give her a whole lot of pleasure, then put a bullet between her eyes. He got hard just thinking about it. Charlie stroked his crotch, then thought about how he would take Naomi.

"Wonder if she's a freak in bed," he said aloud.

In his mind, he decided she was. He decided she would welcome him with open thighs. The more he thought about taking her supple nipples into his mouth, the harder he became. When he stripped her naked in his mind, he was like steel. Charlie unbuttoned his shirt and placed his gun on the floor.

He'd take her on the coffee table first. Then if she liked it, they'd move to the chair. He'd let her beg for her life; then he'd stuff her mouth and explode in there. Charlie had to close his eyes to calm his breathing. Did he have time to masturbate?

He had no way of knowing how much longer Naomi would be. She could come in any moment, and he wished she would because he needed release. He couldn't remember a time he'd been this hard.

Charlie needed to take a leak. He figured that might help ease his tension. He grabbed his gun and pulled himself up and headed toward the bathroom. Damn, he needed to piss like a racehorse.

By the time the first jolt of electricity raced through Charlie's body, he knew the drill. The second one knocked him off his feet. Damn, he'd been caught slipping for real, dick hanging out and his mind on some ass he'd probably never get to hit now.

"Move real slow, 'cause I'm itching to put some lead in your back."

39

If she really didn't believe it before, she damn sure believed it now. Naomi's heart was in pieces when she realized a man had been waiting in her hotel room to kill her. Thank God Detective Jones insisted on seeing her up.

Naomi watched as the brute of a man was being pulled out of her hotel room. Despite being handcuffed, he was thrashing his body all around the hall and grunting at the officers who were trying to get him to the elevator.

"What did he say?"

Detective Jones looked at her. "He won't be saying much."

Naomi turned to him. "What do you mean?" She was beginning to worry more than she needed to.

"He's not new at this. We'll be lucky if we can get his real name from him."

Naomi was horrified. "So you mean to tell me he won't tell us who he's working for? Who hired him?"

Detective Jones shook his head. "Nah, not from

this one. I've seen his kind many times over. He knows the drill. He ain't talking."

Naomi looked away and shook her head in frustration. So they'd never be able to prove who was behind this. She was pissed, but didn't want to take it out on Detective Jones. What if she'd gone up alone? What if she'd . . . She shook the thoughts from her head. "How did he even know I was staying here?"

Detective Jones looked around the room. He wasn't sure why she decided to hide out on her own, but he wished she would've called him to say something. He could've helped her. The detective turned and faced her.

"If I knew who this man was," he began. But the look on her face told it all. She was not about to give up that information no matter what. Since the last time he'd seen her, he'd been busy. From what his investigation uncovered, Sheila was involved in quite a few shady situations, any of which could've cost her her life. She had several arrests for prostitution, and a couple of theft charges on her record. At times Detective Jones wondered how Naomi had even befriended a person like that.

He looked at her again; she was visibly afraid. He wished he had the right words to ease her fear. "It could be anything. When people are powerful, they have access to things we can't even begin to imagine."

"So what should I do?"

"Well, for starters, I don't think you should stay here. Obviously whoever wants you dead knows you're here, and it's just not safe."

Naomi stared at him in pop-eyed horror. She knew she couldn't stay there, but to hear him actually say so was like a slap of reality she wasn't really prepared for.

"Will I ever be safe again?" She didn't mean to ask the question aloud, it was on her brain, but she had.

"Yes, you will. We just need to get to the bottom of this, and we will. Unfortunately, I haven't been able to get approval for your protection just yet."

"Oh my God! Why not? You saw what happened here. What if you hadn't come up? I would be dead right now!"

"Calm down, or try to. I understand. I think this incident will help me plead your case to my captain. I'll get you protection if I have to do it myself!"

Naomi took a deep breath.

"Now let's get you out of here," Detective Jones said.

As she moved around the room gathering her things, she thought back to the shocking moment when they had entered her room and heard someone in the bathroom.

Detective Jones had shoved her back behind him and placed a finger over his mouth, motioning for her to be quiet. His other hand was on his Taser. He caught Charlie completely off guard.

The relief Charlie was experiencing as fluids rushed from his body was indescribable. His eyes were closed as he relieved himself and visions of Naomi danced in his head. Then suddenly a jolt rushed through his body. Then just as quickly another one, and he fell to the floor.

It was too late for him to even react, much less reach for his gun.

"What the—"

A massive knee to his throat followed next, and then it was an uppercut to the jaw. Before Charlie knew what was happening, he was being tussled onto his stomach and he was fighting to regain feelings in his arms and legs. His brain screamed out he had fucked up in a major way, but there was nothing he could do to change that.

"Who are you?" the detective screamed.

Charlie immediately shut down. He knew better than to say a word. Once he was handcuffed, the detective yelled to Naomi, "Call the front desk and tell them to send security up." He then called for backup on his radio.

"You ready?" The question jarred her back to the situation at hand.

"Oh, um, yes. Yes." Naomi pulled the last bag from the vanity and clutched it to her side. Her head was spinning. She didn't know what her future held, she didn't understand how the senator could go from caring deeply about her to trying to kill her in a matter of months, weeks even. She didn't want Detective Jones to see her crying, but she felt so helpless, completely hopeless.

The detective grabbed her suitcase as she managed to carry the other two bags and her purse.

"Where are we going?"

"I haven't decided yet," he said as they walked into the elevator.

"I can't believe this is my life, I can't believe this is what things have mounted up to. It's so unreal."

When Detective Jones pulled up at the hotel in the Galleria area, Naomi wanted to beg him to stay with her. She didn't want to be alone, she couldn't believe she didn't have a single friend or person to turn to. But that was precisely the case.

"Okay, you still have my cell number, right?" he asked as he swung into a parking space.

"Yes."

Naomi watched as he got out of the car and started gathering her bags. They walked into the lobby together, where she registered under a different name.

After Detective Jones helped her get settled into her room, he looked around and said, "You should be safe here. I'll have news tomorrow on some security."

Naomi wanted desperately to beg him to stay. The truth was she wouldn't feel safe until this mess was completely over.

"Well, I'd better get going—"

"Aren't you hungry?" Naomi questioned, desperate to prolong their time together.

Detective Jones stopped midsentence. He wasn't in any particular hurry to go. He was just going to try and figure out who wanted Naomi dead. He figured that was something he could do in a few hours.

"I guess I could use a bite," he said.

"There's a restaurant in the lobby, or we could find something nearby."

Detective Jones shrugged. "Let's go."

Naomi decided after dinner, she'd figure out a way to get him to stay with her.

40

"I can't believe this," Senator Davis said to Big Jim. "She's now at a hotel in the Galleria section." He was holed up in his office closely monitoring Naomi's movement. Whenever she traveled, a small green dot moved in accordance with her position. She was never too far from his reach.

Big Jim wasn't too happy about the new turn of events. Never had he or anyone he worked with had so many problems taking care of business. He dealt with people who made a way when there was none, those who produced results under the toughest of circumstances, and prided themselves on handling difficult jobs. The last thing he wanted to do was let his boss down, and he damn sure wasn't about to do it now, not if he could help it. "As soon as you have an exact address, I'll have someone over there in minutes."

Senator Davis waved his hands about wildly. "I don't wanna hear shit about it. Just do what you gotta do. Now I'm starting to get irritated."

A few minutes later a beeping sound came

from the monitor. The senator glanced over, picked up a pen, then jotted down an address. He ripped the paper from the notepad and stretched it toward Big Jim.

"She's staying at the Westin Galleria," he said to Big Jim.

He smiled at his boss and pulled out a burner. "GPS is something great, isn't it?" He winked at the senator as he dialed the number on his prepaid phone.

The moment a voice answered on the other end, Jim nodded at his boss, then said, "Aey, got a job for you. Need it handled with a quickness." Big Jim walked into the senator's private bathroom. "Here's what we're looking at," he said, and pulled the door closed behind him.

When he emerged from the bathroom several minutes later, he gave his boss a thumbs-up sign and smiled.

Senator Davis eased back in his massive chair and rubbed his face with his hands. He felt a great sense of relief, just knowing that when he woke the very next morning his life could possibly be back to normal. It was a thought that gave him immense pleasure.

"There's a bonus in this for you," he said as his eyes stuck to the ceiling.

"Boss, I just wanna take care of this for you. I don' understand how it's taken this long. Me and Derrick were just talking 'bout it earlier."

Senator Davis didn't want to get too deep into the details of the conversation, he just wanted his problem solved. They had already agreed the less he knew, the better. When Big Jim took a call on his

BlackBerry the senator tried to convince himself again, that this was what needed to be done. And without saying much, he knew his wife was watching each step he made.

"I know you're probably in the office with him, but I was just trying to let you know we need to meet tonight."

41

Naomi sat slowly eating her strawberry swirl cheesecake and racking her brain. She had to try and come up with a way to get Detective Jones to stay with her. She had a funny feeling that she was in far more danger than either of them even considered.

But she didn't want to come right out and ask. The last thing she wanted was for him to think she was some whiny damsel in distress who needed rescuing.

"You sure you don't want some?" She looked up at him and wondered if he knew her game.

When appetizers came, she ate as slowly as humanly possible, then sent the waitress away twice saying she just couldn't decide.

Once the orders were placed, her mind started racing with thoughts of ways she could convince him to stay, but make it appear as if it was his idea.

"You ready to come clean with me?" Detective Jones asked out of nowhere. "Or are we gonna sit here until this place closes and they kick us out? Then after that, what's it gonna be?"

Knowing her jig was up wasn't enough of a reason for her to utter the senator's name. That's when she acknowledged there was still a part of her that didn't want to see any harm come to him. She knew it didn't make sense, she understood the irony in her sad situation, but it did little to change the way she felt.

She didn't want to do anything that might hurt the man who was now trying to kill her.

"You think someone will be waiting in my new room when we get back?" she asked.

Detective Jones shook his head. "Nah, and if there is someone there, I'll handle it."

Naomi put her fork down and sighed. "This is such a fucking mess!"

"Yeah." He nodded. "That it is, a mess for sure."

Silence hung between them.

"I'm doing everything I can to keep you safe, but I feel kinda . . ." Detective Jones half shrugged a shoulder. "I dunno, it's like you want my protection, but I really don't even know what I'm protecting you from."

The disgusted look on Naomi's face when she looked up said she knew he was reaching, but she allowed him to go on.

"Sure, I know all about your friend's plans to squeeze money from these wealthy politicians. I even know about her gambling debts. We've figured out she was gonna use your money to pay off some debt, but she also had something bigger brewing." His eyebrows went up again.

"I've gotta be honest with you about something." He sipped his iced tea, then continued speaking. "The reason it's been so hard for me to get security for you is that my boss seems to think you're a suspect and not a victim here."

Naomi was mortified. Her eyes went from wide in wonder to narrowed and filled with tears.

Detective Jones pierced her with his stare again. "I mean, try to put yourself in my position here. One dead woman who was planning to blackmail some very powerful people with the threat of a paternity suit, and now you just expect me to believe and sell the idea that you were just an innocent friend trying to help another friend and you had no clue what she was up to."

"But I—"

He held his hand up to stop her. "No, let me finish here. So what I'm saying is this, you didn't realize how she was planning to use you, but you had access to twenty thousand dollars for a woman with a serious gambling problem you knew nothing about. Do you see where I'm going with this? Oh, and by the way, you're so scared for your safety, your life, but yet you won't spill it regarding the man who's trying to kill you because you're pregnant with his child."

When Detective Jones scratched his chin, Naomi realized his stubble for the first time.

The way he laid it all out made it, her, sound really bad. He didn't even believe she had nothing to do with Sheila's scam. She had known nothing about what her friend was gonna do. Sheila had told her the press conference would scare the senator back to her; she never said a word about blackmailing anyone for money. That's just not something she would've done.

"I swear to you, I never knew anything about the letters until you told me. I thought I was lending her the money for her mother's operation, I had no idea she was gambling. I know it's hard for you to believe me, to believe this, but the mistake I made was being too trusting. That and . . ." Naomi hung her head low.

"That and falling in love with a married man, that's all I've done, I never planned to blackmail him or anyone else, you've gotta believe me." She knew she was pleading, but the truth was he was her only hope. Naomi tried with all her strength, but the tears still ran down her cheeks. She was embarrassed; she couldn't believe she was still trying to protect the senator. Her safety, and that of her unborn child, everything, was on the line, but still, she was worried about how her actions would impact him and his career. The senator was no longer even talking to her, was probably the one trying to kill her, but still, for some crazy reason, she wanted to remain loyal.

When she looked back up at Detective Jones she didn't even see a hint of softness on his face.

"So, again, tell me why I shouldn't just haul your ass in and make you do what most suspects have to, get a lawyer and prove that you really are innocent. That you are the victim here and not some woman whose partner was killed when she fucked with the wrong person, and now you're trying to save your own ass 'cause you know you're next, and now you trynta play the victim role 'cause you know the dead can't talk."

Naomi buried her face in her hands and started bawling.

42

"She's still not in the fuckin' room!" the senator screamed. He was beside himself. He slapped his forehead and sighed loudly. Big Jim was still at his side. He had tried to calm his boss to no avail.

It had been nearly three hours since the GPS indicator led them to Naomi's whereabouts at the Westin Galleria Hotel. At moments, Senator Davis thought she'd figured out what had happened and ditched the phone, but something else was telling him there was more to it. He and Big Jim stared at the blinking light on the screen that hadn't moved in nearly three hours and they were both on the edge.

"What if she really lost the phone?" Big Jim tried to ask. "It makes no sense that she checked into the hotel, then left for a few hours and is just sitting somewhere near the hotel."

The senator shook his head vigorously. "She still has that damn phone!" That much he knew. Why she was sitting stagnate for hours was crazy to him, but he knew she didn't have a reason to chunk the phone. "Your man would've said she was back in the room.

I don't know what's going on, but that phone is still on her and she's up to something." Senator Davis was near obsessed with this situation. While he and Big Jim were working on the Naomi aspect of this, Derrick was getting a jump start on former Senator Armstrong's aspect of the mess.

He never imagined he'd still be trying to track Naomi down. It had been nearly two weeks since they got to the bottom of what was going on, and still they couldn't take care of the other traitor.

"Why can't we get to her?"

Big Jim jumped up. "I know what to do, let's get an address for where she is now, that spot where the light's beeping still. My guy will go there, let us know what the hell is going on, and then we move from there."

The senator's eyes lit up. "Shit, we should've thought of that two hours ago."

"I'll make the call," Big Jim said as he rushed back into the senator's private bath.

He was glad to be doing something to help. It was nearly eight at night and he still couldn't think of a way to get away from the senator to make his other meeting. Neither had thought this would take this long, but it had. Big Jim was thinking thirty minutes for her to make it back to the room, thirty minutes for the confirmation to come through, but it hadn't. A few minutes later, he stuck his head out of the bathroom, and the senator yelled, "The Grand Lux, 5000 Westheimer Road, right across the street from the mall and hotel."

Big Jim repeated everything he said, gave his guy his marching orders, then turned his attention back to the senator. "Don't worry, we're taking care of this. This shit ends tonight!"

The senator was in his own little world. When Big Jim took another call on his BlackBerry, the senator didn't even look his way.

"You still there with him?" the caller said.

"It may not be tonight," he said, eyeing his boss, who looked like he was deep in thought.

"Call me as soon as you're done with him, I don't care what time it is," Beverly barked.

"Yes, of course," Big Jim responded. He sighed. The senator was right, this shit was getting way out of control.

43

Detective Jones made the man the moment he stepped into the restaurant. He just looked out of place, with his leather jacket and tough features. Instinct caused Detective Jones to touch his piece. Without alarming Naomi, who was still having a meltdown, he let his eyes meet the stranger's and something told Detective Jones Naomi was more victim than she was suspect. He just had a hunch.

Sensing he had been made, the man tried to duck back out of the restaurant, but it was too late. Before he made it to the sidewalk good, Detective Jones had left Naomi, and was jumping on the man's back.

Naomi came running out of the restaurant a few minutes later. A small crowd had formed.

"What the hell is going on?"

"I'm an officer of the law!" Detective Jones yelled to the people who were now gawking at them.

Detective Jones and the man tumbled to the sidewalk. A scuffle ensued, but Detective Jones had the upper hand. He grabbed the man by his arms, which he twisted roughly behind his back, then yelled, "Who sent you?"

"Get the fuck off me!"

Detective Jones jerked the man's arm upward and the man winced, then cried out in pain.

"Who sent you?"

"Fuckin' pig!"

One blow to the side of his head, followed by another tug on his arm, still didn't get him talking.

Detective Jones patted him down, reached for his cuffs, then struggled to clamp them on his wrists. "You ain't gotta talk now. Shit, you dumb ass, you can talk downtown, we got ways of making scum like you talk in our house, buddy!"

"What you holding me for?"

After patting him down again, Detective Jones pulled a gun from his ankle strap and one from the breast pocket of his leather jacket. "How much you wanna bet these aren't licensed? A felon in possession of firearms? Seems to me like you're headed back to that gated community."

Naomi stood dumbfounded. She had no idea how they were able to find her like this. It was really starting to mess with her head. It was something she was doing, but she had no idea what that could be.

As she and Detective Jones waited for a cruiser to pick up the man, she thought about the magnitude of what was going on. It was like there was no place for her to hide. Was she safe anywhere? Would she ever be safe again?

When the two officers showed up, Detective Jones briefed them on what had happened. They read the man his rights and struggled to put him in the back of their patrol car. He was kicking, cursing, and screaming and determined not to make it easy.

"Wow!" Naomi said once it was all over. "How did you even know who he was? You think he was coming to try and—"

"Well, I'm sure he wasn't coming just to say hello!"

"But how'd they find me again?" She was baffled and frustrated.

"You're bugged, 'cause ain't no damn tail that good!"

Naomi's eyes widened. She looked around, then rushed to catch up with Detective Jones. "Bugged? What do you mean?"

Detective Jones, who was nearly at his car, turned and looked at her. "Get real," he hissed.

"What?" Naomi shrugged.

"Look, you keep playing this role and I'm warning you, I'll leave your ass like a sitting duck and we'll see how long you'll last. Either that or you come clean! It's simple, I'm getting tired of this shit!"

"But I—" Naomi began.

"Save that shit! Save it until you're ready to co-operate. You want me to break my back to protect your ass, but you wanna keep me in the dark about what the hell is really going on?" The detective shook his head. "It ain't gonna go down like that. When I leave your ass, either they'll get you or the law will. If I were you, I'd speak up!" he said as they arrived at his car.

Naomi's lips started to quiver. She didn't know why this was so hard for her, but it was.

"Oh, by the way, dump out your bag. Somehow they're finding us and it's gotta be you."

"Dump out my purse?" she asked.

"Yeah, right here. Do it on the hood of the car, it's the only way you'll be safe. Something you've got is leading them right to you, there's no doubt in my mind."

Hoping to please him, Naomi dumped all of the contents from her purse onto the hood of his car.

Detective Jones went through everything as if he knew precisely what he was looking for. He searched her compact, her lipstick tube, the lotion bottle, the old tampons and all.

"See, nothing!" she snapped.

His eyes ran over the items again. This time he picked up the cell phone and closely examined it.

"Wait!" Naomi yelled when the detective plucked the back of her phone off and allowed the battery to plop out. That's when he noticed the little black chip that didn't belong. He put a finger to his pursed lips to keep her quiet, then examined the chip as closely as he could to make sure he wasn't mistaken.

"What the hell?" Naomi couldn't believe it. So all this time, she was being bugged? This was becoming a bit much. Was there anything he wouldn't do to get to her?

Detective Jones reached into his car and pulled out a half-empty bottle of water. He peeled the chip off the phone then dropped it into the water bottle.

"So that's how they've known exactly where to find me," she said in astonishment. "Damn, they are serious!"

"You didn't know?" Detective Jones found that interesting. "So, after all of this, you still don't wanna talk about your mystery man?"

Naomi swallowed hard, then looked the detective

straight in his eyes. "Okay, okay. I'll tell you, but you've gotta believe me when I say I had nothing to do with the scam." She tried to gauge his reaction. "You hear me? I did nothing like what Sheila was involved in and talking about."

"Who is he?" Detective Jones was tired of the games. He wanted this shit over.

Naomi took a deep breath, then looked at the detective without saying a word. She wasn't sure if what she was doing was the right thing to do, but she could tell if she didn't do something soon, she'd really be alone and possibly behind bars.

"Um, Senator Calvin Davis, that's who I was seeing."

Detective Jones didn't have to react; the expression on his face said it all. And shock didn't begin to describe the look on his face.

44

It was nearly eleven that night when Senator Davis finally decided to go home. As far as he was concerned, they'd done all they could and the shit was still out of control. The call Big Jim waited for to confirm the senator's "problem" had been solved never came, and they were thoroughly disgusted.

At that moment the senator decided to let his guys handle it. He was tired. He only wanted to be notified when the deed was done.

"Have the car brought around, I'm driving home," Senator Davis ordered.

Big Jim followed the senator home since he decided he wanted to drive himself. When Senator Davis pulled into the garage of his home, Big Jim took out his cell phone and dialed a number. His evening hadn't gone as planned either.

"Mrs. Davis, I'm right outside. Your husband just went in. Should we wait till tomorrow? This was a long and frustrating night."

"I think it's time we talk as a group. I don't know

what made me think a bunch of men could handle a job that's clearly in need of a feminine touch."

Big Jim rolled his eyes. But her insults were nothing new. He thought back to the moment the senator's wife had first approached him. The conversation was one that left him very uncomfortable, but also very clear about who was really in charge.

"He may sign your check, but let there be no confusion about it, I take care of this career as if it was my own. I'm not taking anything away from my husband, but let's face it, you men, well, you're not always the brightest bulbs in the drawer. Don't get offended, Jim, I'm a straight shooter and what I'm telling you is, we've remained in office this long because I know how to avert problems before they get out of hand. You follow my instructions, and we'll all enjoy the power we've become accustomed to."

That conversation had taken place eleven years prior. Big Jim had been on the job all of sixty days. It was Beverly who told him to find his very best friend and bring him to meet her. Once she met Derrick and determined he would be loyal, Derrick's and Big Jim's lives had changed for the better. Over the years, she had rewarded both men with money, women, and expensive gifts. She told them as long as they remained loyal, they would always have job security.

Sure, the senator probably believed he had hand-selected his security detail, but when it was all said and done, Beverly carefully had a hand in every aspect of the decision-making process.

Now, as he sat waiting for her response, he thought about how correct she had been about just about everything. He chuckled at her theory that men were oftentimes clueless because they thought with the wrong head. Mrs. Davis didn't rub faults in their faces; she merely used them as examples of how things could've been handled differently. At times Derrick was a bit bothered by what he called her meddling, but he too grew to understand she had all of their best interests at heart.

"We'll meet tomorrow. The senator has a block of time where he'll be busy. I'll come to you."

"Yes, ma'am," Big Jim said to the dial tone.

Inside the Davises' house, the lights stayed on until the wee hours of the morning. Beverly Davis was in one of the guest bedrooms. She'd been trying to figure out the best way to clean up her husband's mess.

When the senator didn't come to her door, she slipped on a silk robe and made her way down to her husband's study. There she found a glass of brandy next to his head, which was lying on top of his arms on the desk. She had a right mind to leave him sitting there, so he could wake with a serious crook in his neck.

"Calvin?" she called out to him.

There was no response.

Her heart skipped a momentary beat. She hoped he hadn't gone and done anything stupid.

"Calvin?"

This time he stirred, but didn't fully respond. She stepped all the way into the study and glanced around. It had been a while since she was inside his study. She felt a bit ashamed at how she herself had allowed this situation to mushroom into what it had.

Beverly and a few of her peers had long ago decided the best way to handle their husbands' indiscretions was to spearhead them and remain in control.

But never before had any gotten so out of control and so beyond repair. She decided she'd meet with the other ladies in the morning before she went to Big Jim with what their next step should be.

Once she decided her husband was just drunk, she flicked off the light in his study and went back up to bed.

45

"So you see, that's how it happened, that's how we met, and now here I am."

Naomi told Detective Jones the entire story about how she came to be Senator Davis's mistress. She described it from the very beginning, when the senator's wife came to the school, months before her husband, to meet with each and every staff member, herself included.

"So, did she come first as a prescreening process?" Detective Jones asked.

Naomi shrugged. She never really thought about it that way. She remembered how many of the teachers chuckled at the extent some women went to help out with the family business, and they left it at that.

"What do you plan on doing now? If your friend hadn't been killed, what was next for you?"

Naomi shook her head. It was still so hard to believe Sheila was dead, and even more difficult to believe how she had had it in for the senator. After Naomi spilled her story, Detective Jones had a story of his own to tell.

"I can't believe she was trying to play both sides," Naomi said.

"Well, believe it, because she was. And I don't think it was a lack of loyalty with her. She had a problem, she would've sold out her own mother if she thought that would result in more money. I've seen people do crazy things as a result of their gambling addiction."

"But I thought I knew her so well," Noami admitted regretfully.

"You can never really know everything about a person. Sometimes you can know a person all your life and still you won't know all there is to know about them. People share with you want they want you to know and that's it. You shouldn't feel bad about that. I think now we've gotta figure out a way to keep you safe . . ."

When Detective Jones's voice trailed off, Naomi looked up at him. "What are we gonna do?"

"We've gotta go talk with the senator, together," he offered.

But the horror on her face told him how she felt about that idea. Naomi couldn't bear facing him now that she knew what had been going on right under her nose. For all she knew, he probably thought she was working with Sheila. She felt a mixture of sadness and embarrassment.

"No! Absolutely not!" she screamed. "I came clean with you to prove I had nothing to do with Sheila's plan, but I am not about to face him after all of this." Now it all made sense to her. That's why he behaved the way he did, he gave her the cold shoulder because he was on the defensive, and now she understood he had every right to be.

"What a mess!" she added.

"It is a mess, but what do you want to do? Keep looking over your shoulder? You want to continue to move every week? And what happens when your baby is born? What will you do then? You plan to raise your child and live in fear?"

She had never thought about it that way. "But if he knows that I've told you the whole story, I just don't know what . . . he's gonna be so mad at me, so disappointed."

"The man is trying to kill you!"

Naomi heard what he was saying, she'd witnessed the two men who came to do God only knows what to her, but still, deep inside she had issues believing the senator would allow any harm to come her way. It just didn't seem real to her.

Suddenly a thought popped into her mind. "If Senator Davis thought I was working with Sheila, wouldn't Senator Armstrong have thought the same thing?"

"I suppose so," Detective Jones answered, wondering just where she was going with this.

"Well, so we don't know for sure that it's Senator Davis, do we?" Naomi held up a finger. "Just hear me out. Whatever she promised his camp, do they not still want it? I mean, especially if they paid her, they're looking for the information she promised, right?"

"Okay," he agreed.

"So for all we know it could be his men who sent those guys after me." Her voice clung to some hope. Despite the skepticism she saw on his face, she knew she had given him something to think about.

"Okay, for argument's sake, let's say it was

Armstrong's men who were after you. You think they just wanted to talk? And how would they benefit from killing you? If anything, he'd want you alive because he would want you to tell him everything you know about the man who kicked him out of office." Detective Jones stopped speaking for a moment, to see if anything he said had registered.

"I suppose you're right," she admitted somberly.

"Look, I know you don't want to believe this man would ever do anything to hurt you, but the truth is, he saw this as his survival. People with power, they're not like you and me. They will do whatever it takes to remain in power. You and that baby of yours are the only obstacles for him. For all you know he's probably got higher aspirations, and he sees you and this kid as a threat. I'm telling you, that's what this is really about."

Naomi didn't want to believe it. She knew his words rang true, but she had meant more to the senator than anyone could ever understand.

She didn't even attempt to stop the tears that gushed down her cheeks. Her heart was hurting and she didn't care who knew. It was close to one in the morning. Detective Jones had moved her to a different hotel, after they dropped off the bugged cell phone at his office.

"Will you stay with me?" she asked through sobs.

He looked at her, but didn't answer right away. He hated to see a woman cry, but he also hated women who acted so naive. Why couldn't she understand what was so plain to see?

"I can't keep protecting you if you're not willing to step up and help yourself," he said firmly.

Naomi started sniffling. She was torn, she didn't

know what to do, she didn't understand how she had gotten caught up in the middle of a political nightmare. "What do you want me to do?"

"I want you to let me handle this. You do what I tell you and don't ask any questions, trust that I'm taking care of everything."

Naomi simply nodded. She was so tired of running and questioning whether she'd see another day.

"Agreed?" Detective Jones asked for clarification.

"Agreed," she said.

"Okay, why don't you go take a nice long, hot shower? I've got to figure out a few things, but trust me, you've made the right decision."

Moments after the shower went on, Detective Jones pulled out his cell phone. He looked toward the bathroom before dialing the number he knew by heart.

"I've got her, she told me everything, and she's ready," he whispered into the phone.

46

The next day things moved at a marathon pace around the Davis house. Beverly was up before the sun and had been working the phones ever since. It took a little elbow grease, but she had finally secured Penelope Armstrong's personal cell number. The two women had gone back and forth for nearly an hour, when finally Beverly told Penelope she felt a face-to-face meeting was necessary.

The wives agreed to meet at three for tea and Beverly moved on to the next item on her list.

"Jim, I need to know what Derrick was planning to do with regard to the Armstrong situation," she said into her phone.

"Um, I was handling the other angle," Jim stammered.

"Jim, this is no time for games. Once the senator is dropped off, I want to see you and Derrick here no later than noon today, understood?"

"Yes, ma'am."

Beverly wanted to be prepared for her meeting with Penelope. She knew the older woman was still bitter because her husband had lost out on a position in which they'd hoped to retire, but Beverly wasn't afraid to refresh Penelope's memory about some things that her husband might have forgotten. Once she dealt with the guys and Penelope, she planned to deal with her husband.

Beverly wasn't sure if she was going to opt for the straight-and-narrow solution, or the one that required some dirty work on the parts of everyone involved.

"Men!" she hissed, thinking about this mountain of a situation that should've remained a molehill.

Later, when she confirmed her husband was in the meeting, Beverly put her plan into action. First she made sure she'd have at least fifteen minutes alone with Penelope before the rest of the wives showed up. Beverly had her driver take her to their bank, where she went into her safe-deposit box and removed several large envelopes. Next she pulled the DVDs she had hidden in a small box, then headed back home.

She was there for ten minutes before the guys called to say they were outside. Beverly checked her reflection in the mirror that was always favorable, then adjusted her three-strand pearl necklace and answer the door herself.

"Mrs. Davis," Big Jim greeted.

"Come in, fellas." Instead of stepping aside, she allowed them in, then walked out of her front door to glance around. When nothing seemed out of place, she came inside and met Big Jim and Derrick in the sitting room.

"I don't have a lot of time, but I wanted to let you two know I'm now handling this situation. I've already been on the phone with the press, both here in Austin and in Houston. I'll give them more of what they want later. But for now I needed to inform you that you are to abandon whatever plan you were working on for my husband and wait for more instructions from me."

"Even the Armstrong situation?" Derrick wanted to know.

Big Jim knew better than to question her. He listened and spoke when she paused, indicating she wanted to know if he understood. Usually he'd respond that he did, and things would continue to flow nicely.

"Yes. Even the Armstrong situation. I'll have news for you fellas later about how to proceed next. But I can assure you, from here on out we will all proceed with caution. This isn't as simple as my husband thinks it is. No one will harm Ms. Payne, not now and not later. That would just make things more difficult for us all, and I'm sure you all agree with me that no one needs difficulty, correct?"

"Correct," Big Jim answered.

"Yeah," Derrick reluctantly agreed.

Once she escorted them out, she rushed upstairs and changed into one of her signature sweater suits. She kept her pearls on, then flipped through the stack of envelopes and DVDs she had. When she found the one she wanted, she rushed downstairs and prepared to meet with Penelope Armstrong.

Beverly dipped into her stash of imported teas and ordered finger sandwiches to be delivered right before her scheduled meeting with Penelope.

Thirty minutes into Beverly's meeting with

Penelope she realized the woman was trying to play hardball.

"So let me be sure I understand your position here," Beverly said between pinched lips. "You're saying to me that you're not the least bit repulsed by what your husband is attempting to do all in the name of trying to reclaim his state seat?"

Unlike Beverly, Penelope wasn't born with a silver spoon in her mouth. She enjoyed the years she had spent as a senator's wife and wasn't too happy about her husband being forced out of office. She knew her husband was working to find dirt on Senator Davis, but she had no idea he had even been successful. If Beverly was looking for sympathy because her husband had risked his career over a piece of ass, she was talking to the wrong person.

"I have control over my husband, Beverly. My mother always told me a real wife trains hers properly. It's no secret what you and Calvin have done all in the name of keeping your marriage fresh, but how you choose to handle your personal affairs is up to you. Don't try to tell me how to handle mine."

Beverly hadn't expected to have to play her trump card so quickly, but she was always prepared and this time was no exception.

"I don't think you remember when you were a member of the club yourself. I was afraid it would get to this, but . . ." She slid one of the envelopes toward Penelope.

At first the woman turned her nose up at it. When she reached toward the table, she picked up her teacup instead of the envelope.

"Go on, I think you'll be interested in what's inside. I mean, if you're not ready to help me fix this problem our husbands created in hopes that you will reclaim your spot, I need to make sure you understand the lengths I'm willing to go to protect mine."

When Penelope opened the envelope and pulled out the first of several pictures, her hands began to tremble. Next it was her quivering lips that let Beverly know she had finally had a change of heart.

A few minutes later, the tone of their meeting had changed. Beverly was grateful for the new attitude; she finally felt like she was making headway. Once she and Penelope had come to the agreement that Beverly and no one else would deal with the press, they kissed cheeks like old friends at the door and promised to visit again.

By the time the other wives arrived, Beverly had all of her ducks in a row. All seven who had received Sheila's letter were there and they were just as nervous as Beverly had suspected they would be.

"Ladies, it's time to take care of this matter once and for all."

Theresa Johnson spoke up. "I heard that we're in this peculiar situation because of a few husbands. Why must we all suffer?"

Theresa was a heavyset woman with raspy reddish brown hair and pale skin. She had no fashion sense and very bad acne, for which she insisted on using a home remedy that didn't seem to be working.

"So you think it's time to branch out on your own. When there's a problem and you come to us for help, we should remember your position here tonight, then?"

"That's not what I'm saying," she stammered.

Beverly's features were pinched. She wondered

why some women had to make things more difficult than necessary.

"Well, I don't know about you, Theresa, but I know what my husband's been doing for the past seven years, and like Beverly, I don't need to get burned to know that fire is hot," Amy Taylor confessed. "I say if any of us are at risk as this letter indicates, I think it's time we put our heads together and come up with a solution. So if you wanna handle things on your own, go'n, girlfriend, but, Bev, you can count me in, honey. What do you need me to do?"

"Me too," another wife said.

Three others nodded.

"I'm in."

All of it was music to Beverly's ears. "Now, like I said, I have a sweetheart of a plan!"

47

The next day, Naomi and Detective Jones were having breakfast at a restaurant close to his substation office near the Montrose and she was already starting to feel better about her situation. The relief she felt was similar to what she had experienced when she finally revealed to Sheila that she was seeing the senator.

"Got some appetite there today, huh?" the detective asked jokingly.

"Yeah, guess the baby is really hungry this morning."

"Well, eat up." He smiled at her.

After a few more minutes of silence, Naomi started thinking about the fact that Detective Jones still hadn't told her about their plan. She had no clue about exactly what they were going to do.

"So who made the first move, you or the senator?" Detective Jones asked, and caught Naomi completely off guard.

"What do you mean?" she asked, this time putting down her fork. Something about his question rubbed her the wrong way. The more she thought about it, where was the added security she was supposed to have by now? He said he only needed to convince his boss of her innocence, but he still hadn't said a word about it.

"I was just wondering if you came on to him, or he to you," the detective added.

"Yeah, but what's that got to do with anything? And when are we gonna go talk to your boss? You believe me now, right? I mean, nothing has changed since we last talked right?"

"I'm gonna talk to my boss. And yes, I believe you, I don't think you intentionally set out to blackmail anyone. But the truth is, Senator Armstrong is still trying to find you. He believes you could be the key to ending a political tug of war."

"I see."

"I know you never envisioned your affa—um, I mean your relationship with the senator would lead to all of this, but this is where we are right now."

"But you're not telling me what you believe we should do, what we're gonna do. They're trying to kill me, the other ones want me to win a seat, I just want everyone to leave me alone! I want this nightmare to be over. You said you were gonna help me, why aren't we going to the police department? Why aren't we talking to some sort of task force or something like that? I'm so confused."

When the next words fell from Detective Jones's lips, Naomi thought she had lost her ever-loving mind. He couldn't be serious!

"What would you say about meeting face-to-face with Senator Armstrong, just so you could hear him out?"

Suddenly Naomi used her eyes to start glancing

around the restaurant. Her instincts had kicked in, telling her she needed to get away from him and she needed to do it quickly. The bathroom, if she made it there, she could possibly slip out the door, get away from him, and go find some real help.

"Um, meet with Armstrong? You think that's what I should do?" she asked nervously.

"Well, I thought more about what you said. If Davis really is trying to kill you, trying to reason with him won't be much help," he offered up.

"But what about the security we talked about?"

Naomi watched Detective Jones squirming in his seat. When his cell phone rang, she looked at him, grabbed her purse, then said, "Take it, I need the ladies' room anyway," and got up.

Instead of going to the bathroom, Naomi took advantage of the crowd heading into the Breakfast Klub. She slipped out of the restaurant and rushed around the corner. Naomi didn't waste any time; she hopped on the first light rail train approaching. She kept looking over her shoulder and out the window, but never saw Detective Jones coming. She wondered if he even realized she was gone. When the train took off, she released a sigh of relief. She was tired.

Something wasn't right about him, but she wasn't about to stick around to find out how he was planning to betray her. She had heard him on the phone the night before. She had snuck out of her shower draped in a towel when she realized her bath gel was still in her bag. His words gave her temporary pause; it sounded like he was reporting to someone about her, and it didn't sound like his boss.

At first she thought it was just paranoia sinking

in. As she stood beneath the hot water, she tried to explain what she had heard away. But his question about Armstrong this morning confirmed her suspicion and she had been through enough to know things would only go downhill from there.

Naomi jumped off the light rail in the museum district, then hopped on a bus and headed west. When she got off on Highway 6 and Westheimer, she went a few blocks, then checked into the first hotel she saw.

After pacing for a little while, she started going over her options, and there weren't many.

"Okay, I could try to go back to Austin and talk to the senator, tell him I know why he treated me the way he did. I could accept his apology and tell him everything he wants to know and beg him to take me back so we can go from there. He could leave Beverly, and we could make a go of it."

The more she heard herself, the more ridiculous she knew she sounded. The truth was, the senator probably wouldn't see her, much less talk to her.

Her only other option was to go through with the plan Sheila had discussed with her. Maybe she could contact the press, she could do everything they talked about except blackmailing these people.

"That's what I can do. I can do the press conference myself, I can get on there and tell the world that I'm pregnant from a married senator, one who abandoned me when I told him I was pregnant."

Her decision was made, but first, she needed to go by her apartment. She figured going at night no one would see her and would be a safer move. Naomi had no way of knowing how that decision would change the course of her already crazy life.

48

Big Jim's heart nearly skipped a beat when he heard keys dangling at the front door. He and Derrick thought he'd be in Houston for an entire week trying to figure out how to track Naomi down. He put his hand on his piece as he waited in the dark.

His instructions were very clear.

"Go to Houston and do what you have to to bring her to me!"

"But how'er we gonna find her?" Derrick had asked in frustration.

Big Jim took his marching orders and was prepared for his trip to Houston. He decided to start at her apartment and figured if need be, he'd wait her out no matter how long it took.

But it looked as if he wouldn't have to wait for long. Moments after he heard the keys at the door, it opened and in stepped a visibly pregnant Naomi. Big Jim was behind the door. She walked in, flicked on a light, and walked to the back without ever even noticing him. He put his gun away, deciding he didn't need it. He heard her moving around in the bedroom, and when she finally emerged and saw him, she dropped the papers she was holding and froze, but she never screamed or said anything. She stood staring at him in wide-eyed fear.

49

"A-a-are you gonna kill me?" Naomi asked
nervously. She remembered the man well. He was
one of Senator Davis's bodyguards and he had
probably been sent to kill her personally since the
other two couldn't finish the job.

She swallowed hard and waited for his answer.

Naomi thought about how foolish it was for her
to return to the apartment. Anyone could've been
waiting for her, either one of Armstrong's men, Detective Jones, or this big brute of a man who stood
before her now. "Well, are you?"

When he shook his head, saying no, she thought
for certain he was trying to trick her. Of course
he was gonna kill her, that's the only possible
reason for his "visit." She looked at his menacing
face and wondered how much she would suffer
before she died. Naomi began to take slow steps
backward.

"You're coming with me," he said.

Naomi stopped walking. "So you're gonna take

me somewhere else, and kill me there?" she wanted to know.

"I'm not killing you at all. Pack a bag, I'm taking you to Austin, on the jet," he said.

Naomi's eyebrow shot upward. "You're taking me to Austin?"

"Uh-huh." Big Jim nodded.

"On the jet," she confirmed.

"That's right."

She tossed him a skeptical look, then sucked her teeth. "Yeah, like I'm just gonna buy that one."

"Look, we can do this the hard way, or we can do it the easy way. It's up to you, but I'm not leaving Houston without you." He shrugged. "Alive," he added.

"Are you serious?" Naomi didn't know what to believe. What if this was just another trick, another attempt to lull her into a false sense of safety? She knew she was outnumbered despite the fact that Big Jim was alone. He didn't do a thing without being instructed by the senator, so she knew that's why he was lying in wait inside her dark apartment.

She was so tired of running, so tired of wondering if every stranger was out to do her harm. She wanted so desperately to believe in someone who wasn't just lying to her.

"Look, lady, if I wanted to kill you, you'd be dead, believe that!"

He had a point. That much she understood.

"So you're not trying to kill me?"

"What are you? Five foot four, maybe 120 pounds? If I wanted you dead, we wouldn't be standing here talking about it. Believe that!"

The look in his eyes touched her to the core, but

she wasn't afraid. He wouldn't need much to get rid of her if in fact that's what he wanted to do. As a matter of fact, she thought, he could've just put a bullet in her before she even turned on the light.

"I can pack a bag?" she questioned, still not sure if he could be trusted.

He nodded. "Yup, pack a bag for about two days. I'll even bring you back home."

"Then you're gonna kill me?"

"Look, I'm not killing you!" Big Jim realized he was damn near screaming, but she was starting to work his nerves.

"C'mon, girl! Get your stuff and let's go!" he said.

"Can we get something to eat before we get on the plane?"

Big Jim sighed and rolled his eyes. *Women!* "If you get your stuff and we hurry, we can grab some food before we get on the plane, yes, but we need to get going now."

Naomi decided she would take her chances with Big Jim. If she later learned her decision was wrong, she figured there was nothing much she could do about it because if he wanted her dead, she would be dead by now.

Once packed and ready to go, Naomi walked back into her living room. She glanced around the place as if she was trying to take a mental picture.

"Whassup?" Big Jim asked.

"Look, I know you say you're not gonna kill me, but I'm wondering if I can just leave a note here, you know, for my cousin just to let her know where I'm going. I lost my cell, so I can't call her," she said.

Big Jim knew there was no cousin, but if that's what she needed to get things going he figured there was no harm in doing that.

Naomi grabbed a notepad and pen.

Wendy,
I'm going to Austin with Jim, Senator Davis's
bodyguard. I'll be back by Tuesday at the latest.
Call me if I'm not here by then.
Love,
Naomi

"You forgot to put the number on there," Big Jim said, looking over her shoulder.

"Oh yeah," she said as she quickly scribbled the senator's number on the note. That's when she realized there was no way Jim or anyone else from the senator's camp was going to kill her.

They stepped outside and walked down the block to meet the town car. When Big Jim held the door open for her to climb into the backseat, she took a deep breath.

She eased into the car and he followed behind her. Naomi had no way of knowing Derrick was waiting outside her building so he could go in and clean up the place. That note she left for Wendy was one of the first things he got rid of.

"So the senator finally decided he wanted to see me, huh?"

"Nah." Big Jim shook his head.

Alarm gripped Naomi's heart. "What? I thought you said we were going to Austin. You said the senator sent you to get me, and that you weren't gonna kill me. Now you're going back on your word?"

"Look, chill, I never said the senator wanted you. I'm not gonna kill you, and we are going to Austin, but it's the senator's wife who wants you, not the senator," he said.

Naomi's eyes widened and her mouth dropped open.

50

By the time Big Jim checked Naomi into her room at the Holiday Inn near Highway 35, she was ready to conk out. The emotional roller coaster she'd been on seemed so unreal.

"I'm in the connecting room right next door, so don't even think about making a run for it. And if you decide to try, Derrick will be out in the hall to help change your mind."

Naomi sucked her teeth and rolled her eyes at him.

"You tricked me," she hissed.

"I didn't trick you. I told you we were going to Austin on the jet, and that I was not gonna kill you. You're still alive, right?"

"But you didn't tell me I was going to meet with Calvin's wife!" she yelled.

"Look, lady, I'm just doing my job! You didn't have to come, you came 'cause you thought the senator had sent me. I ain't got nothing to do with that."

Naomi was fuming mad. She didn't want to meet the senator's wife, again. When she first met her,

Naomi wasn't sleeping with the woman's husband, but now this was surely to be a very uncomfortable meeting. And what did Beverly Davis want with her anyway?

After Big Jim left, Naomi did something she couldn't imagine she would. She picked up the hotel phone and called the senator's cell phone.

She was shocked when his voice rang out in her ear.

"Hello?"

She paused a bit. "Um, Calvin, Senator Davis?"

He didn't respond right away. She wasn't sure if he was going to hang up on her or not. After a few minutes of silence, she spoke again.

"I know you don't want to talk to me, but—"

"Where are you?" he asked, interrupting her.

"You mean you don't know?"

"Know what? I don't have time for riddles."

"I'm here in Austin, at the Holiday Inn off 35. You mean, you didn't know?"

"Who brought you?"

"Your bodyguard, how could you not know?"

"What's your room number?"

She didn't know if she should answer right away. "Are you gonna kill me?"

"I love you, how could I kill you?"

Naomi rattled off her room number and less than an hour later, her hotel room door was being opened. She was in bed, but not alarmed at the sound of the door opening.

When their eyes met her heart melted all over again. It was like a dream she was having after all she'd endured over the last few weeks. She didn't even know how to behave in his presence.

He stepped toward her. Her hair was ruffled, she was wearing a dainty nightdress, nothing sexy, just simple. But the senator couldn't remember a time when he'd seen her so beautiful.

"Don't say a word." He removed his jacket and loosened the buttons on his shirt. When he stood before her in only his boxers, she pulled the sheet back, inviting him in to lie next to her.

They embraced in bed, held each other like lost lovers reunited. Then their lips met and it was like fireworks exploding. They kissed and petted each other like teens high on hormones.

Naomi had dreamed of this moment, but she still felt she was trapped in a surreal world. When he took her nipple and squeezed it, then moved to the entire breast, she felt herself flood with warmth.

"Oh God, Calvin!"

"I love you!"

She shoved him down, climbed on top of him, and kissed from his neck to his chest to his stomach, to his thighs. Naomi took his swollen member into her mouth and welcomed it and him home. She savored his juices, rolled her tongue around his muscle, and massaged him vigorously.

The senator clutched the sheets and gritted his teeth. This was what he had missed so very much without her. She knew just how to love him, she knew all the right spots to hit, kiss, and taste, and it drove him nuts.

He was like steel when she mounted him and wiggled her hips to work her way down.

"Oh, Jesus!" He grabbed her hips and helped guide her until his steel wand vanished deep within her warmth. "Oh yessss!"

He grabbed and palmed her breasts with force.

"Oh yesss, baby, yesss! I've missed you!" Naomi was screaming and she didn't care who could hear. She had no idea when she would have her senator again. When he thrust upward to try and hit her spot, Naomi squeezed him tighter. She wanted to drain him, she wanted everything he had.

Nomi rode him like their bodies were made for each other. In the night, her screams of passion rang out loudly, but they were music to the senator's ears.

They loved each other for more than two hours. The senator gave her the intense kind of pleasure he did when they were first together. He exploded in and on her so many times they lost count. When they finally collapsed for the last time, Naomi was spent and ready for sleep. She wanted nothing more than to wake wrapped in his powerful arms.

"Ssshhhh," she heard him whisper.

"Where are you going?" she whined.

"I shouldn't have stayed this long, I've gotta run."

Naomi rubbed sleep from her eyes. She couldn't understand. While they were in the throes of passion, she thought everything was gonna be okay. He didn't want her dead, he said he loved her, and now he was saying he shouldn't have stayed? This was the part she wished was a dream.

She eased upright in bed and watched in horror as the senator walked out of the room and probably out of her life one last time.

51

Beverly knew exactly where her husband had been when he came sneaking into the house at 5:45 in the morning. She was no fool, that was for certain.

"Men are so fucking stupid!" She couldn't believe he would go back to her after all he had at stake. If it wasn't for her, they would've lost that seat years ago.

She didn't get much sleep that night, but that was okay with her. Once her husband was home, she fell back to sleep, then woke a few hours later.

"Are you joining me for breakfast?" Beverly asked as she shuffled down the hall, ready to get her busy day started.

When she didn't hear a response as she passed the senator's room, she pulled the door open and realized he wasn't in there.

She rushed downstairs and heard his voice booming from the study. He was on his cell phone.

Beverly didn't bother inviting him to breakfast. She went to the kitchen and notified the chef that she'd be having breakfast out on the deck.

"It'll be ready in twenty minutes, ma'am," he said.

Although she wondered who her husband was on the phone with, she didn't feel like addressing him directly. The conversation they had had about the mess he created did not go the way she envisioned it would.

"I can handle my own affairs," he had screamed.

"Are you crazy! Your affairs are what got us in this fine mess we're in. Now I have to fix what you've fucked up, I don't understand why you can't just keep your damn pants zipped!"

Senator Davis knew better than to engage his wife in a yelling match about his infidelity. He did make a mistake, he fell in love with Naomi. She was everything he wanted in a woman, but he knew they had no future together. Beverly wouldn't allow it no matter what. She'd go to her grave before she'd see him with another woman as his wife.

"Are you finished?" he asked with a tight jaw.

Beverly stormed out of the room and prepared for the next day. She felt like she only had one shot with Naomi. And because of the pregnancy, she knew she had to tread carefully.

Beverly began to get concerned because she didn't understand why her husband was still in the house. Didn't he have someplace to be?

She didn't want to all but kick him out of the house, but she was expecting company in a matter of hours, and the ladies had things they wanted to do before the "guest of honor" was due. Beverly walked back toward the study again.

"I'll be there in thirty minutes!" she heard her husband scream.

Beverly felt relieved. She walked back up to the

guest room and gave her items a once-over again. She was a bit excited about the pending meeting of the minds.

When her husband left the house, Beverly immediately started calling around to remind everyone to be on time. She was having sandwiches delivered and they were drinking mimosas.

This was going to be an inquisition, but it appeared more like a party, just the girls getting together for a little chat.

52

Naomi was sluggish and dragging and she knew it. She was in the midst of misery and paying dearly for the unexpected romp with the senator the night before.

When Big Jim banged on her door, she wanted to scream to him to leave her alone.

"You need to get ready to go!" he hollered.

"Go away!" Naomi yelled back.

"You got an hour if you want food," he warned.

She buried her head under the pillow and struggled to revisit the ecstasy she had shared only hours earlier with the senator. The truth was, she didn't really want to go and visit with the senator's wife a mere few hours after she had loved her husband.

Naomi got up, showered, and tried her best to dress as conservatively as possible. She applied a minimal amount of makeup and fingered her tussled hair. She didn't want to be sexy, alluring, or anything else that might make this woman hate her even more. As she walked down the hall, Derrick and Big Jim stood when they saw her.

"Long night, huh?" Big Jim commented.

Naomi didn't care what they said. If the senator came to her again, she'd take him and enjoy every moment of it. It didn't matter to her what the hired help thought.

They rode in silence to a sprawling estate near Lake Austin. Derrick was driving, and Big Jim sat with her in the back. She didn't know if these two thought she was gonna make a run for it or not.

"When did you get in?" Jim asked Derrick.

"Oh, this morning, caught a red-eye," he answered.

Naomi looked at Jim. "You said he was outside my door, in case I tried to run," she hissed.

"Yeah, I know what I said." He smirked.

Naomi was disgusted with them both. She rolled her eyes when she heard Derrick laughing at how they had once again fooled her.

"Are we at the right place?" Naomi asked the moment they pulled into the circular driveway. She looked around and was curious about the other two cars. Suddenly she wondered what was going on.

"This is Senator Davis's house," Big Jim said.

"Yeah, but why are all these cars here?" Naomi turned in her seat to look around again.

The guys shrugged their shoulders. They were just told to deliver her; they didn't ask questions, simply did what they were told. Besides, they both knew whatever was in store for her was probably gonna be worse than what the senator would have done. He was the one with a heart in that marriage, but neither had the courage to betray Beverly Davis.

Naomi stood at the massive oak door. Her heart was doing somersaults the way it flipped and jumped around in her chest. She didn't want to be there, she wanted to be back in that hotel room with the senator.

She turned to look back at Derrick and Big Jim in the car. When Jim's eyebrow inched up she took a deep breath and used the knocker to knock on the large door.

It didn't take long for the door to swing open. A petite woman stood in front of her. Her face was frozen between a smile and a frown.

"Yes?"

"Um." Naomi shook her head. Shit, that's not what she meant to say. "I'm here to, um, my name is Naomi Payne," she finally finshed.

"Yes, how do you do?" The woman stepped aside. "I'm Beverly Davis, thanks for coming. Come on in, we're in the sitting room," she said as she allowed Naomi to walk into the foyer. Naomi could feel her eyes burning into her, but she knew she was in no position to protest or turn back.

To the left was a grand winding staircase. A few steps into the house, they were standing beneath a massive chandelier, and for the first time, Naomi realized they weren't alone. She heard voices mixed with laughter coming from a nearby room. So much for the intimate little chat she thought she was about to have with Mrs. Davis, she thought.

Naomi waited for Beverly to say something else, tell her which way to go, or to maybe say they were going to meet in private on another floor or something. To Naomi's surprise, Beverly was stunning. She was poised, and behaved like an honor student from charm school. She was wearing a bone-colored sweater suit. The skirt fell right above her knees, and the top hugged her curves. Her makeup was tasteful, and she wore diamond studs in her ears, with a large matching diamond tennis bracelet. Naomi tried not to stare at the massive rock on her ring finger, but she couldn't miss the dazzling stone.

This was not a good idea, she decided before she even walked through the doorway and saw the sea of faces staring back at her. Naomi looked at Beverly, who still stood near her side.

"Ladies, this is Naomi Payne," she announced as if she expected applause.

"What is going on here?" Naomi asked, her eyes still on the women in the room. She watched them as they watched her and whispered to each other. She noticed when a few of them smirked, others frowned. She hadn't signed up for this.

"I'm leaving," Naomi said.

"Why?" Beverly asked sweetly. Naomi turned to her.

"I'm not sure what's going on here, but I'm not about to sit in a roomful of strangers, I thought you wanted to meet and talk with me in private. This is crazy!" Naomi turned to leave.

"Ms. Payne, we're all interested in talking to you. See, seven of us received threatening letters saying our husbands fathered your child." Beverly glanced down and allowed her stare to linger at Naomi's belly.

"You and your friend, your late friend, were planning to blackmail us for cash, so I think the least you could do is humor us," Beverly suggested with a smirk.

Naomi held up a shaking finger. "I had nothing to do with that. I had no idea what Sheila was up to until the police told me after she died."

"Sure you didn't," someone tossed in. Naomi looked, but she couldn't tell who had said it.

"She didn't die, sweetie, she was killed," Beverly corrected with satisfaction.

"If you guys think I'm about to sit here and be attacked by a roomful of angry women, you've got the wrong person," Naomi said to Beverly.

"No one's angry. I was just hoping to avoid a huge media mess. I figured if we talked, you could get a little relief, regain your life, the life as you knew it, and, well . . ." She turned to the room. "My friends, you can't help their curiosity. They just hoped you'd humor us, you know, give us the mistress's perspective."

Just when Naomi thought this thing could get no stranger, she chuckled and looked at Beverly. She thought back to the fact that the senator had come to her in the middle of the night after basically sending men to find her. She was a fool for him, she couldn't explain her love, she couldn't understand why she had even agreed to meet with his wife. It was obvious this woman was deranged.

"So, you're, um . . ." She looked back at the women before turning her gaze to Beverly. "You're telling me you knew, um, I mean you know about me?" She couldn't hide her shock.

"Knew about you? Darling, I all but hand-selected you. Of course I knew, know about you, there've been so many yous I don't know how I keep up."

Naomi blinked back tears. She knew what Beverly was up to and she wasn't about to break down in front of her or her friends. She swallowed hard, then looked again at the women assembled in the room.

"Fine, what do y'all want to know?" Naomi asked defiantly.

"Please, have a seat, we could be here awhile," Beverly said sweetly.

"Oh no, I don't need a seat. I don't plan to be here awhile. I don't have to prove a thing to you or anyone else. If you already knew about me, I don't understand why I'm here," she said.

"Well, because when you and your girlfriend set out to blackmail us, you ladies changed the way we play the game. I don't think there's a woman in here who doesn't know her husband's dick's been elsewhere, but none were stupid enough to knock someone up, then allow the mess to threaten his career."

"Who here would leave her husband because of an affair?" a woman asked.

When Naomi looked around the room, not a single hand was in the air.

"Power is just a magnet for extra ass," another woman said. "You get used to it."

Naomi bit her lip. These women couldn't be serious, she thought.

"I must admit, Calvin has never developed feelings for any of his little hoochies," Beverly said.

"Oh, one year a woman crashed our vacation, told me she and Steven were going to be married later that year, said he was leaving me to be with her," a different woman said.

"I've heard that one before," someone else tossed in.

Beverly looked at Naomi. "Now, don't tell me you believed Calvin would leave me. Chile, they all promise they'll leave." She shook her head, then sipped from her crystal flute.

53

Senator Davis couldn't believe what he was about to do. His life might as well be over. But the truth was, he was caught in a serious sling. Beverly had him by the balls, and there was very little he could do. He kept going over and over in his mind just what he had agreed to. Each time he thought about it, he only hoped he'd be able to go through with it because if he didn't Beverly would have his head. And she'd make sure her father would take care of what was left of him. He really didn't want to do what she had suggested any more than he wanted to have to leave Naomi.

"You think you've fallen in love with her, and that alone has put everything, our family, your political career, everything we've worked so hard for at risk. You can't see it, but trust me, you've left us vulnerable. Oh, the stupidity!"

He didn't respond, because deep inside he knew she was right. He couldn't explain what he felt for Naomi, the way he had fallen for her, but he knew how much his heart ached without her.

"You remember Jennifer? What about Kenya, or Tameka? Carine, she was my favorite, all but told me I'd soon be replaced, you remember them?"

The senator remembered them all, but he didn't appreciate Naomi being placed in their category. She was different. He knew he could never leave Beverly, but if Naomi understood, and she agreed, he could see himself building a future with her; that was before the baby. A baby, he told himself, was too difficult to explain.

His other children, a boy and a girl, fourteen and twelve, were tucked away in an exclusive boarding school. Beverly said it was best for them. But he didn't know if "them" was the children or him and her. Would a baby have really been that detrimental to his career? He knew the answer to that question, he knew he'd be ostracized and escorted right out of the capitol, but in his mind he imagined hope. He just wasn't brave enough to take the risk. His mind traveled to his earlier conversation with Big Jim.

"So what's going on?" the senator had asked him.

"She's trippin', had me drop Naomi off at the house," he had said.

The senator tried not to act surprised. He knew his wife was meeting with Naomi, but he felt to have Naomi over to their house was very cruel. But he was not about to play into his wife's warped game.

No matter what he tried to focus on, his mind lingered to what might have been happening at his house. Should he go and try to rescue her? Did she even need his help? Maybe Beverly was working things out the way she usually did. He knew despite his concerns and worries, his wife would never do anything that could make fascinating headlines or front-page news the next day. That much he didn't have to worry about. But still, he was curious about just what might've been going on there. And what man wouldn't be? It wasn't every day his wife had his mistress over to the house for tea.

Senator Davis leaned back in his chair and looked out the window. He wondered what life would be like if he didn't have his powerful position, if he didn't have to answer to his constituents, or if he could just do whatever he wanted, live like ordinary people.

He had grown to despise his wife. As he rolled her idea, or her orders, around in his head, he came to the realization that it wasn't worth it. Senator Davis had really been struggling with the choice he was being forced to make. But he was not about to let anyone get the last laugh on him.

When he was done, everyone including Beverly and her highbrow daddy would understand that only he had control of his destiny and what his outcome would be. His mind was made up, he was going to do it his way.

54

"So it was you all along?" Naomi could hardly believe what she was hearing. Beverly Davis, the wife of a prominent senator, her lover, the father of her unborn child was the one who really wanted her dead!

"Dear, you need to learn to play your position. It's what you should've done all along. You're not very wise. If the senator meant as much to you as you say, you would've understood what a threat you had become."

"But I—"

"You what? You thought you and the senator would run away together?" another woman interrupted. She started laughing, as did a few others.

Naomi's heart rate began to increase. She had thought it was the senator all along. She thought he was trying to silence her, but she had been wrong.

Before she could do anything she was shoved down onto a chair. When she tried to get up, strong arms shoved her back down again.

"Don't fight it, dear, there's really no point."

"What?" She struggled a bit. "Why?"

"Because when you mess with one of us, you mess with us all. When we finish spinning this tale, the truth will come out, the truth being that you tried to blackmail us after being rejected by a married man. Quite surely no one will believe your little story of innocence."

"But I didn't—"

"Yes, we understand," Beverly said as she stepped closer.

Naomi felt herself getting light-headed; she was fuming. She was getting so angry. Suddenly her heart began to race so fast she was afraid it might leap from her chest cavity.

"Now you can go," a voice said.

On wobbly legs she stood, and tried to command her legs to run toward the door. She took a few uncertain steps. When the stinging sensation tingled in her back she was confused. Sure, she heard the banging noise, but it didn't startle her. Then she felt wetness right before she closed her eyes.

Her body hit the floor with a thud.

Beverly picked up the phone and dialed 911. When the operator answered, she used a frantic voice to say, "My name is Beverly Davis, I just shot an intruder, please send someone quickly."

The women scrambled out of there just as they'd planned and discussed.

"Are you gonna be okay?" one of the wives asked before she fled the scene.

Beverly shook her head. "Yes, now go, they'll be here soon."

"Don't forget the letter," she told Beverly before she scrambled out the door.

In the seven minutes it took for the Austin police to arrive at the Davis compound, Beverly had her speech down to a tee.

The officer came in and looked around.

"Mrs. Davis, are you okay?" he asked. He had already been warned about the level of importance of this call before he stepped foot inside the house.

"I am, I just think, well, I don't know where she came from, I was here alone and all of a sudden I hear someone, I didn't even think to ask. After everything with the letter, well, I guess you can say I'm a little on the edge."

"Yes, we understand, ma'am."

The officer saw the body lying facedown near the foyer and sent his partner to talk with Beverly Davis. Soon there was a knock at the door.

He stepped around Naomi's body, once he confirmed there was no pulse, and opened the door to three women standing there.

"We heard what happened, can we talk with Beverly?"

The officer looked dumbfounded.

"Tammy here is an attorney," the woman tossed in. "We need to see her right away."

The officer stepped aside.

In front of the officer, Tammy looked at Beverly and said, "Is this the woman who was trying to blackmail us?"

Beverly looked at her, then at the body. "I don't think so. I mean, I don't know, but Calvin was having trouble with a stalker," she answered.

The officer was taking notes the entire time.

"Ma'am, there was a stalker? And who was trying to blackmail you?"

"She's not saying a word until her attorney arrives," Tammy said to the officer.

He shrugged. He wasn't sure what was going on. The last thing he or his captain wanted to do was arrest the wife of a state senator. He already knew that in the state of Texas a property owner has the right to protect his home. As far as he was concerned, Mrs. Davis had done nothing wrong.

55

Two Months Later

Beverly Davis watched from a nearby corner as her husband concluded his news conference. It had taken some time, but she and her father had convinced him this was the best way to deal with this matter. And the timing couldn't be better. The grand jury had rendered its decision and it only made sense.

At first, Calvin had the nerve to say he wanted to leave! He was gonna try to salvage his career after a divorce; that is, until Beverly's father explained to him just exactly what he was planning to give up. This was gonna be Calvin's last term in state office, but not because of the scandal or any other.

After a two-hour meeting with his father-in-law, it was decided that the Davises would seek higher office. With his father-in-law's money, and his squeaky-clean image, the Hollywood politician was going to aim for the U.S. Congress. Early polls had already predicted his victory.

"At this time I will take only a few questions

from reporters," he said, as he nervously shifted his weight. Senator Davis had just completed a news conference in which he announced that a Travis County grand jury had decided not to bring charges against his wife. He made a brief statement, quoted his wife, then opened it up for questions from the press.

"Senator, this woman, was she a part of the plot to extort money from seven state senators including yourself?"

"At this time all I can say is investigators are looking into that. My wife, as well as the wives of my colleagues, have confirmed receiving a letter, but we have no idea where that letter originated, and I'm not at liberty to say at this time what that letter contained."

"Is it true that you had a stalker situation on your hands?"

The senator glanced to his left. After his attorney slightly shook his head, he turned back to the microphone.

"That's a question I cannot answer at this time," the senator said.

"Next?" he quickly added.

As he waited for the next question, he thought back to the conversation he had had with his wife after he learned what had happened at his house.

"She wasn't even pregnant!" Beverly had screamed. "Can you believe that? They were trying to blackmail us with a paternity suit and there was not even a child!"

"But you had to kill her?"

"Listen to yourself! You risked our entire lives,

our future on some little tramp and now you stand here questioning me? As if I'm the villain here?"

"She was harmless!" the senator shot back, shaking as he spoke.

"She was out to blackmail us, all of us! She wasn't pregnant, look, see for yourself!" Beverly tossed a pregnancy test toward him. His eyes registered on the negative sign, but he refused to believe it. It couldn't be true. As the senator's eyes fixed on Beverly, she went in for the kill.

"I'm tired of cleaning up your messes! How could you not even suspect that the little tramp might be up to something?"

The senator rolled his eyes. He was tired of this crap, of Beverly's crap.

"My father said—"

The look he had shot in her direction told her just how he felt about whatever it was her father was saying this time.

"Senator, are you going to retire?"

The question snapped Senator Davis back to the press conference. He looked at the reporter who had asked the question; then he tilted his head forward. "That's it for now, thanks so much for your time."

As reporters tossed additional questions toward his back, the senator walked quickly off the stage and into the wings where his wife and a few others stood waiting.

Detective Jones couldn't believe how close he had come to being able to retire early. When he was first approached by the Armstrong camp, he told himself there was no way in hell he'd risk his job.

But the more he talked with David, the more he was convinced things would work out fine. He had been staking out Naomi's house for several days before he finally got the news.

"That's bullshit!" he screamed to his superior. "She was involved with Senator Davis, she told me herself! I'm telling you he killed her!"

Detective Jones's boss got up from his chair and closed his door.

"Let this one ride, Sergeant," the older man said to Jones.

"Whassup?"

"These people play by different rules. When you've got money, your problems aren't average. The suits are handling this one personally, so we're out of the game," he added.

"I think they killed her, Captain. That girl didn't break into the senator's house."

"Ain't the story the wife is telling," the captain said as he walked back behind his desk. "She said, and a grand jury believed, your friend there was obsessed with snagging herself a lawmaker, staked out their house, and when she thought no one was home, worked her way in. The missus, who was home alone and running late for a bridge tournament, claims she just heard a sound, feared for her life, and shot first."

"And lemme guess, thanks to Governor Perry's recent move, it was all legal because this was a stranger in her house, right?"

"Protecting her property. You got it," the captain confirmed.

Detective Jones sighed. "I just hate that that girl and her baby had to die like that."

"Baby?" the captain asked.

"Yeah, she was pregnant," Jones offered up.

"Nah, not our chick. There never was a baby, all part of the plan." The captain shook his head. "This shit reads like one of them lifetime movies. Either way, it's done and over with. Trust me, we got enough shit to keep us busy."

When Detective Jones walked out of his boss's office, he thought back to how Naomi had him so convinced. He actually believed her, and all along she was playing him, playing them all.

Once Detective Jones was unable to deliver, he never heard from the Armstrong camp again. He decided it was just as well. In the past few months much of what he believed wasn't even real. Now when he watched political commercials he always wondered what secrets the candidates were hiding. Then he'd smirk and thank God he was done with that gritty world.